Additional Praise for The Monotonous Chaos of Existence

These stories recall the rhythms of poetry, offer up the intimacy of memoir, and often feel more like films than fiction. *The Monotonous Chaos of Existence* got me thinking about similarly semi-surreal and ecstatic truth tellers Denis Johnson and Chester Himes, a comparison that will have to do for now because I'm still dizzy and not exactly thinking straight after reading these interrogations of the cruelty and absurdity of occupation and so-called post-colonialism. Clear-eyed personal/political storytelling that is exciting, askew, and challenging.

—Brandon Soderberg,
coauthor, *I Got a Monster: The Rise and Fall of America's Most Corrupt Police Squad*

"I'm tired of turning the dials of History," declares the narrator of one of these elegant, genre-crossing reveries, as if time were a type of mechanical function. On the contrary, *The Monotonous Chaos of Existence* proposes that time is a web of competing histories, fragmented memories, alternative realities, and dystopian dreams. A virtuoso of literary entaglements, Hisham Bustani is the spider at the center of this impassioned display of literary weaving.

—Campbell McGrath,
author, *XX: Poems For The Twentieth Century*

THE MONOTONOUS CHAOS OF EXISTENCE

Hisham Bustani

Translated from the Arabic by maia tabet

MASON JAR PRESS | BALTIMORE MD

Originally published in Arabic as al-Fawda al-Ratiba lil-Wujud (Beirut: Dar al-Farabi, 2010). All the rights to the Arabic original and English translation are held by the author.

Published by
Mason Jar Press
Baltimore, MD

Printed by Spencer Printing in Honesdale, PA.

Learn more about Mason Jar Press at masonjarpress.com.

CONTENTS

NOTE ON TRANSLATION

This translation was carried out in collaboration with the author. Several edits from the original Arabic were made in order to enhance flow or smoothly convey meanings and contexts; also, the sequence of the stories differs slightly from the Arabic original. All these modifications have been approved by the author.

Many of the endnotes are the author's and appear in the original text; the translator's notes are specified as such.

THE MONOTONOUS CHAOS OF EXISTENCE

Entry Point

Who are we? We find that we live on an insignificant planet of a humdrum star lost in a galaxy tucked away in some forgotten corner of a universe in which there are far more galaxies than people.

—Carl Sagan

DISTURBANCE

CITY NIGHTMARES

[The building that sees, hears, and speaks]

The building is dark and gloomy, full of ghosts from the past. They wander around, in and out of apartments and rooms, and up and down the stairwell. Like people, the building can see and hear, and it can also speak: its eyes stare out of the windows and from the cracks in the walls; it listens through the downspouts of the rain gutters and from the bathroom windows that open onto the ventilation shaft; and it speaks...oh, how it speaks.

"Bitch!" "Bastard!" I could hear my uncle and his wife scream on the second floor, their endless disagreements like an old broken record. Then came the sound of shattering glass and slamming doors, and the building shuddered like an old refrigerator.

I was always alone. Every day, I'd sit on the stairs outside, as if I were waiting. I waited for a bus to take me far away, but the bus never came. Once, I envisioned it falling from the sky, but it was just a tile that had fallen so close it brushed up against my scent before crashing to the ground and breaking. I recoiled like a loaded spring and looked up: there was no one up there, and the roof wasn't even tiled. I would remember that later, when tiles rained down from the sky.

They were hitting each other. My uncle was up to his ears in debt, and his wife was expected to keep up appearances. But the wall cracked, the nail was dislodged, and the picture shattered...frame, glass, and all. Tiptoeing past her slumber-filled eyes, Uncle fled his wife, his creditors, and everyone he knew. He went to Cairo and died there.

That morning, you could hear a mother beating her children, and when she came out of the building, purse in hand, I was still sitting on the stairs in front, waiting for the bus.

To top it all off—the children's wailing and the mayhem—she spat on me.

[The bus that never comes]

It is green as green pastures, the doors don't close, the windows are glassless, and the seats are made of Damask roses. Its passengers are all friends of mine: Dante, Stendhal, Yann Tiersen, Mourid Barghouti...oh, and it is full of cats, and birds too. Driverless, it runs on wheels made of music, and there is no conductor.

At every stop, they all disembark, spread out a rug, and sit around with glasses of wine and wedges of cheese, as well as garlic labaneh and seeded whole-wheat bread. They keep a trash bag close. The soldiers toss in their rifles and boots, the informer his eyes and ears, the bougie lady her high heels, the pupil his teacher, the opportunist his position, the prostitute her society, and the Almighty Leader his very self.

Only then do they all raise a toast to love and freedom. They bare themselves, detail their failings, their traumas, and their hang-ups, and become one copulating body in a grand orgy before scattering back to their separate selves, climbing hand in hand aboard the bus, and going on to the next stop.

But the bus never comes.

[The ghost room]

Oh, my, how that building spoke...

My widowed grandmother lived on the ground floor. She'd lost her husband before I was born and had stayed on in the building even after all the other residents had left.

"I made friends with the imprint of their fingers on the wall plates and with their dust bunnies under the armchairs. If I leave, I won't have anything left of them. Like this, at least their ghosts remain."

"Here is where my first child fell and bled, and here, on top of this wardrobe, is where your father hid from his father after he'd broken the window and caught sight of the black belt in the furious fist bent on finding him."

She would skirt around the corners and the pieces of furniture and tell stories. The second floor brought on a torrent of tears. "I will never see him again." That's what she said when he stole away to Cairo, and when he died there. Only one room at the far end of her apartment remained closed. She never spoke about it or let me go near it.

Sometimes, I managed to give her the slip and would go and glue myself to the keyhole. I could barely make out the sound of a labored and pained voice, but no words.

One day, when I couldn't stand waiting for the bus anymore and my stomach was growling, I went to find her, but no one was on the ground floor. "Teta, Grandma," I called, wondering where a barely ambulant old woman could go, and how she could have passed me—I'd been at the door of the building since morning.

The house was spotless, its floors and walls gleaming. No dirty fingerprints on the electric switch plates and no dust bunnies under the armchairs. Everything looked spanking new, as if it had been wrapped and the wrapping had just been taken off. And the door to the forbidden room lay open.

I approached, tiptoeing, and was startled by the darkness and the deep and wordless moans. As my eyes grew accustomed to the dark, my grandfather appeared, sitting by the bed like the arches of an ancient aqueduct, bent over double, his head propped in his hands, his fingers squeezing his eyes as he suppressed a feverish sob. On the bed lay a small, immobile, black figure: a charred and desiccated me.

With memories of mouse rooms, ghost rooms, as well as the dark under-the-stair closets and their accumulated terror, I darted out of there, running from the apartment and out through the door of the building onto the street.

[A fleeting visit to what once was]

I ran out of the room, out of the apartment, out of the building door and onto the street, panting, my pulse pounding like the drums of war, throbbing through the veins of my hands, my ears, my temples, feeling as if I was going to explode. For a second, I pulled myself together and looked behind me—there I was, all in black, standing at the door of the building. As soon as my eyes met my eyes, my ghost ran after me, and I almost fell. Night descended suddenly, and I slammed into a high wall.

"It's the end of the road," shouted a gravelly voice.

I turned around and found that I was face to face with myself. Adrenaline rushing, pupils fully dilated, I began to shake; while

I was silent as a stone, immobile as a wall overgrown with vines, features erased and tinted lemon yellow.

I was struggling to open my eyes, desperate to wake up, but it felt as if invisible fingers were holding them tightly shut. I managed to pull together every bit of strength I had left. I transformed it into a chisel and a hammer, which I banged so hard that my eyelids opened. *Aaahhhh*, I gasped, sucking all the air out of the room. I burst into tears and began sobbing.

I felt so sleepy. I was dead tired but didn't want to go back to that room, on that street with the wall blocking it, to that other me, and the feeling that I couldn't open my eyes. I was shaking like a leaf.

••••••

She heard children's voices far away. She brushed away her tears and looked out of the window. There were four of them, coming out of their school overlooking the Qal'aa near the hawuz on Jabal al-Lweibdeh, wearing shorts made by capable mothers who passed them down from sibling to sibling. The sign read: School of Islamic Sciences—founder Tayseer Dhibian. This is now 1946.

The children trotted down the dirt road toward the Tash orchard, and when they reached the stone enclosure, they jumped the wall. They filled their empty little bellies with green almonds or figs—filling their pockets while they were at it as the day was still long. They crossed over to the other side of the orchard, leaped over the wall again and out onto an open space that overlooked Wadi Saqra, with Jabal Amman rising behind it. In the little clearing, they lined up their stones and split into two teams. She heard them crying out, gird-ou-sharah. She didn't know that game.

Once they were done playing, they sat on the edge of the bluff, looking into the distance at the Circassians' ox-drawn carts making their way up the dirt road that traversed the orchards and wound around to Wadi al-Seer all the way from the city center. They got back up to play, standing on the rocks and boulders, rolling those they could dislodge from the top of the hill down into the bowl of the valley, uncovering a spider, snake, or lizard. Lizards had pride of place among the reptiles: painted on the palms of the children's hands, their blood was a palliative to the teacher's rod.

As the sun began its descent on the horizon, the children went looking for nature's candy—the furqo' they delighted in eating. By the time the sun had gone down behind the mountains, they had gathered mallow, dandelion, and hawkweed, wild greens they would have for dinner—their mothers' injunctions would not be ignored.

When they got back to the hawuz, and before each boy went his way, the four of them turned toward her and waved goodbye as they melted into the gathering darkness.

She closed her window and peacefully dissolved into a deep sleep.

[When tiles rained down from the sky]

I was still sitting in front of the building door, stark naked and waiting for the bus, with nothing to toss into the trash bag before climbing aboard, when the sky darkened. The clouds were unlike any I had seen before: white and steely, so low you could see their particles, and it made you want to sneeze...their thunder an endless crashing of sheet metal.

It was only seconds before the first drop fell: a tile that shattered beside me on the ground. "But the roof isn't tiled," I thought to myself. Before I could finish the sentence, down came another, then a third, and a fourth...then a torrent of tiles, cut stone, window glass, and flying pieces of furniture.

I ran to get away from the downpour, crossed the street, and jumped onto the neighbors' balcony. I looked across the way: lifting off the ground was a thick gray fog that shrouded everything.

As the cloud dispersed, a yellow monster with metal jaws and big elliptical rubber feet sat atop the building, or what was left of it.

He winked at me from the glass eye at the center of his small head, raucously belching out a plume of smoke. The sky was overcast again with the same kind of clouds I had just seen for the first time...and that same metallic crash of thunder.

[Downtown]

Welcome! Welcome to Abdali!

Gaping holes in the ground and narrow metal cranes rotating on their axes hoisting concrete slabs and stacks of breeze blocks and steel.

Welcome to what is slated to become Amman's new downtown. Amman has no old downtown for it to have a new one. Amman used to have a city center. But now, in the era of big-box stores and packaged things, Amman is to acquire a downtown, possibly even a Centre Ville, like Beirut's. The umbilical cord between them is the same: Solidère Beirut and Solidère Amman are one. The same Hariri silken glove destroying and "developing" in order to line the same pockets with billion-dollar profits—the difference only in whose pockets are being lined, and the cuts and contracts that ensue.

Welcome, welcome to Abdali!

All along the periphery of majestic Jabal al-Lweibdeh, bulldozers had set to work. The project was extended even before the land had been expropriated. It was all planned in advance, like an act of God, an inescapable stroke of fate.

Amman's mischievous children used to roll boulders and rocks from Jabal al-Lweibdeh to the bottom of Wadi Saqra, dislodging the snakes, spiders, and lizards underneath (at a time now long gone). Whenever they found a new friend under one of the rocks, they squealed with delight, their little feet scurrying to chase after it.

Today, it is rocks and concrete slabs that hurl people down from the mountaintop—with memories, histories, and photos shattering in the plain below. And no sooner are the old houses brought down than everything below is pulverized by a colossal footstep, leaving in its wake a crater dozens of meters deep.

Welcome, welcome to Amman's new downtown.

Behind the huge multi-color banners ringing the area with images of a delusional future, there's nothing but dust, excavation sites, and cranes—and workers trucked in from faraway places whose sweat is wrung dry with impunity.

A blistering sun beats down on the leveled land, now devoid of trees, of people, and of memories; enveloped in rays of gold, a lovely young woman runs, terrified and directionless, as though pursued. She stops suddenly. "The building was here," she says, then starts running again. She stops once more. "No, it was here." She runs and runs and runs. The building was here...no, here...or rather, here.

Soon, someone is pursuing her: a security detail in charge of guarding the project. What does she want, they ask, catching up with her. What is she looking for?

"For the bus stop where the bus never comes," she replies, out of breath.

NOTES:

The **four friends** were Abdel-Hadi Shuqayr, Abdel-Fattah al-Bustani, Mohammad Khamis, and, his brother, Shafiq Khamis.

The **Tash orchard** on Jabal al-Lweibdeh was a grove of fruit trees that belonged to Mohammad Tash. It was eventually razed and its green expanse covered with residential buildings.

Gird-ou-sharah, Monkey and Emblem, was a popular game among Amman's children.

Jabal al-Lweibdeh, **Jabal Amman**, and **Jabal al-Qal'aa** are three of the seven hills on which modern Amman was established. In Arabic, *jabal* is a mountain and *wadi* is a valley, hence **Wadi Saqra** and **Wadi al-Seer** are two of the valleys between the hills. **al-Qal'aa**, the citadel, is a walled site atop one of the seven hills, which dates back to the Bronze Age. It is dotted with the remains of Byzantine, Roman, and Umayyad buildings, including an Umayyad palace, a temple dedicated to Hercules, and a Byzantine church (translator's note).

[MUSEUM OF FOUND OBJECTS: DISCARDED PHOTO ALBUM 1]

An Indian laborer found these photos in a torn-up album in the rubble of the demolished building. They were placed in safekeeping at the Archaeological Museum in Jabal al-Qal'aa. The captions, written in blue ink on the back of the photos, are reproduced below.

Mohammad Khamis (first row, first from right); Shafiq Khamis (first row, second from right); Abdel-Fattah al-Bustani (first row, second from left); Abdel-Hadi Shuqayr (first row, third from left), with Akram al-Khatib, their teacher (center), in front of the School of Islamic Sciences.

The School of Islamic Sciences scout troop, including the four friends. The school building is visible to the left.

A visit by the venerable Sheikh Tayyib al-Aqabi al-Jaza'iri to the School of Islamic Sciences. To his right is Sheikh Nadeem al-Mallah, and in the back, on the top right, and wearing a tarboosh (fez), is the school's founder, Tayseer Dhibian.

Abdel-Hadi Shuqayr (R), Abdel-Fattah al-Bustani (L), friends.

Abdel-Fattah al-Bustani in front of the hawuz on Jabal al-Lweibdeh.

FREE FALL IN A BROKEN MIRROR

She's hanging horizontally above a lake. She can see the whole of herself reflected on the surface of the water. The reflection is blurred every now and then by ripples forming and expanding outwards. She feels bitter and sad in alternation as she watches it. She tries desperately to run away or turn upside down, or even just stand upright. But she remains fixed in place, as if anchored by invisible ropes.

A dense fog rolls in and she is glad, even happy, about the lack of visibility. It feels to her as if she's been turned inside out. Her cute, short hair comes into view, along with her two ears, each adorned with seven little earrings. Her perfectly feminine body, enveloped in the fragrant aroma of lemon, emerges before her eyes.

A chasm appears as the fog lifts. The invisible ropes break and she falls, still horizontal, faster and faster, until she shatters in the pit below.

•••••••

She lifted her head off the pillow and felt around with her hand. Yes, she was all there, in one piece, the fabric still draped on the chair across from her. It was just an ordinary piece of fabric, at times gaily colored like the happiness of children and at others plain, like the black standards of the conquerors. Whatever the circumstance, the material was fluid as water and sharp as a knife-edge—a razor blade plunged from the top of her head deep into the cleft of her thighs.

She got up, placed the piece of fabric on her head, coiling herself around it like an adder, almost choking as she wound it about her neck. She looked at herself in the mirror: the seven earrings disappeared from view and her short hair became invisible. *You're not me,* she told the reflection in the mirror, wondering whether the appearance of things was really their foundation. She answered the question categorically: "Other than for hypocrites—and there are *so many of them*—form is an expression of substance."

When she opened the door, people were milling around the iftar table: Father, Mother, brothers, sisters, neighbors, relatives, everyone from the neighborhood, the entire town was there... *so many of them!*

She gritted her teeth.

• • • • • •

The light above her was a large multi-colored ring. In alternation, the colors twinkled like stars or looked like one of Mondrian's paintings. Every once in a while, from the opening, the heads of people who knew her appeared, calling out to her.

"That's where you will stay," she hears her father say, "in the pit." And her ears pick up her mother's muffled sobs. She averts her face.

She tries to climb out of the pit, digging her fingernails into the walls around her, to no avail. No sooner does she touch the walls than they turn into jelly and she pushes and pulls against them in vain.

[*Argentinian tango for one*]

Empty space is the canvas, and the body is both paintbrush and pigment. The right half begins to move, arm wrapping gracefully around the back of the left half, hand pressing lightly, inviting her response. She responds and the music of the bandoneon swells up in the background. But there is no one there beside herself: just her, and her again.

In the glow of the twinkling colored lights, the two halves fuse, shoulders squared, torso taut. Only legs and feet move, agile and deliberate, as though pivoting on an axis. Her legs wrap around one another, intertwining like the limbs of adjacent trees, lingering for just an instant before effortlessly unwinding.

The tango dancer comes out of the wings, strides purposefully toward her, and her again, hand extended. "No one can do this dance alone. It takes two to tango." She stops, turns toward him, and places her hand in his. But her two halves won't come together and she keeps tripping over her own feet.

"Do you know how similar we are? I love dancing with a passion. When I throw my body into the beat of the rhythm, I don't see myself as being swept up by its pulse but as jousting with it. It's like sex, but even better. I can come over and over again, and feel as if I'm exuding a magical, spellbinding energy. There's something about it that defies explanation. It's like I'm in a Sufi trance, except that the thread keeps breaking...I've been to the ends of the earth, to Argentina itself, and I still can't figure it out. Does a spell remain a spell once we have decoded it? Could it become even more magical, maybe?"

"And maybe not..." says her left half. "Once they realized what was going on, they flipped my life upside-down like one of those hourglasses: 'Your going to study overseas is out of the question. Look at you: now, and you're like this. God knows what would become of you if you traveled outside.' What outside, what nonsense? The fool doesn't realize that I turn myself inside out right here, every day. He doesn't realize that the filth of his mind is enacted thousands of times behind that mendacious veil of piety. Being one of the prostitutes on Jean Genet's balcony would be more honorable!"

"Do you realize how similar we are?" he said, leaning forward. He pulled her up after her two halves arched back, out of sync, over his arms. "You have no idea the passion with which I love dancing. When I went to my first tango class, I was drenched in cold sweat as I got out of the car. Me? Dancing? What if someone saw me? What about my social standing, my respectable job, my connections who would never understand? I stole up to the third floor and picked the only studio with a wooden door for my private lessons, all the other studios had glass doors. It took me six months to drum up the courage to join a group class. And now, one night a week I shed all the layers and masks, cohere into this form, and dance until I'm dizzy. Before dawn breaks, I put all the layers and masks back on, and evaporate, so to speak, vanishing into thin air."

When he turned to complete the motion of wrapping his leg around hers, he stumbled, which was odd—he wasn't a mere beginner or a wannabe. How could someone in search of the holy grail of dance, who had mastered a body that shaped empty space, stumble like that? "I want to see *one* body and four legs," he heard the maestro's voice saying.

Holding her hand in his, he pushed her back lightly and was surprised by the gap growing between them. He was amazed that it grew both on the side and behind. He looked out from the corner of his eye and saw that his other half was calmly moving away with hers. “How similar I am to you...”

As the music swelled, there were four halves dancing.

• • • • • •

“You’re gray, or, to put it better, you live in these gray zones: you’re afraid of soaring and falling, afraid of confrontation, and you spin around the center, slowly breaking apart. You’re gray in the stance you adopt, living in two worlds, veiled with your parents, and unveiled with everyone else. Gray also in love, neither getting close enough for me to kiss you nor far enough away for me to forget about you. And even in your studies: you don’t like your major but pursue it with the mind-numbing monotony of a government job. And also gray in your job: you toil for a paycheck, not for the sake of being creative or contributing something, or even for pleasure. You’re dizzy, like a dancer who pirouettes without keeping her eyes on a fixed point. And you’re making me dizzy in the process.”

She put down her glass of orange juice and sat up in her chair looking at him. “Everything in its own good time,” she said smiling. “You can’t rush things. When the time is right, I *will* rebel, I’ll throw that piece of cloth in all their faces and live as I please. It’s more complicated than simply standing up for what I believe and going on my way. I’m not worried about society’s harshness toward me. This tender skin, which you’re always looking at with longing—you think I don't see it in your eyes—" she added, winking at him, "can turn thick as a sharp-toothed alligator's! I don't want that harshness to be directed toward my parents."

"………."

"Do you know," she went on, looking straight into his eyes, "when I was telling my mother my dreams, she blurted out, 'I'd rather die than witness the misfortunes you will visit upon us.' Just think," she added, choking up, "my dreams are misfortunes, and my mother gasps, practically choking on me, as if I'm suffocating her."

He covered her hand with his. "History doesn't move forward by hanging on to the past," he said, "and the right time doesn't just happen. We make it happen. By the time the right moment arrives, your rebellion will be superfluous. The moment will have passed. The right moment doesn't come about without being ushered in. You should be pursuing your dreams and realizing them rather than chasing after society's mirages and your parents' visions."

"I have only one dream left: to leave this country."

[Gray young woman pursuing shadows with a gray young man]

He's sitting on the verandah wall made of stone, the orange streetlights glowing behind him and casting his shadow on the wall opposite. Taking short, quick puffs from the cigarette smoldering between his fingers, he's thinking about her.

She sits across from him on a chair, saying nothing. Her seven earrings are twinkling in the dark as she looks at him.

He waves his cigarette hand in the air, and his shadow on the wall does the same. The shadow of the cigarette starts climbing up her body, its gray edges hovering by her eye.

The poet once said: "Even when lit by fire/The shadow remains gray, neither male nor female."

Suddenly, the edge of the shadow glows ember-red and she screams: her hands fly to the side of her face where her right eye burns.

•••••

The right half: "Calm down and listen to me. We've been arguing with Father and Mother, we're at odds with each other, and that scoundrel burned my eye. We can't go on like this. As the saying goes, if the mountain won't come to Muhammad, Muhammad must go to the mountain. How would it help to rebel? It's futile. It'll mean heartbreak for them and a headache for us. They're our parents, they love us deeply, and we don't have anyone in the world besides them. Come on, it's just a piece of fabric: let's wear it and be done."

The left half: "I have a spirit, a mind, and convictions of my own. I want to shape the world and be shaped by it as I please. Am I here only for others to write my narrative, for them to subjugate me? I might agree, if they were rational but they are the very epitome of un-reason. That'd be a terrible defeat."

The right half: "Let's emigrate, then. They won't let us travel to study, I know, but we could find a young man, a suitor, one of those who return to the old country in search of a bride to take back to the new country. We'll marry him and it'll be our ticket to freedom."

The left half: "And jump from the frying pan into the fire, from one patriarch to his doppelganger? What if that dungeon turns out to be even darker than the one we're in now?"

The right half: "Ohhhh stop, will you! We've got to get out of this hole at any cost. You're killing us."

The left half: "You're the one killing me. And if I die, it's over for you too."

•••••••

She's hanging horizontally above the chasm. She can see her two halves fighting below. She feels bitter and sad in alternation as she looks at them. She tries desperately to break away, to turn upside down, even to just stand upright. But she remains fixed in place as if anchored by invisible ropes.

NOTES:

“I want to see one body and four legs,” is a line from the film *Tango*, by the Spanish director Carlos Saura.

“Even when lit by fire/The shadow remains gray, neither male nor female” is a verse from *Shadow*, a poem by Mahmoud Darwish.

SLOW BREAKING OF LONG-TERM BONDS

She is totally alone, just as he had been after his friends betrayed him. His appearance in her dreams eases her terrible solitude, but she ultimately has to wake up and face life not knowing whether it is the life she has chosen. She doesn't want to know.

[Books@Café, 2008]

"Do we choose life or does it choose us?" she was asking. "Do we create our own destinies, or do we simply make our way patiently and submissively according to some pre-ordained fate?"

When she raises her eyes from the glass and meets his gaze, she knows the answer, and she knows that her questions don't amount to much. As if she's poking a tiny hole in what is the brick wall of her powerlessness—an illusory hole, at that.

"If only I could erase everything behind me, if only I could live in the present moment, here, without having had a life I didn't choose."

Did she mean what she was saying? If she hadn't chosen that life, then who had? Was she just some invisible shadow, mere uncondensed vapor?

"I loved music, especially the violin. What a divine instrument it was, its four strings could carry me so far away without ever breaking. I'd managed to get a scholarship to study in Budapest thanks to a communist friend I'd met at university. She had been on the side of the revolution, the one whose red flags are dyed with the sweat of laborers and peasants toiling for the attainment of their sacrifice. 'You'll fill our new lives with melodies,' she had said. I was so happy I was floating on a cloud. I was in seventh heaven. But they all said no. Who? My father's brother, my mother's brother, our relatives, the entire clan, all of them came crawling out of some damned hole just to rip the pages of my life apart. 'What's that you want to study, music?' they said. 'So you can end up working with dancing girls and crooners and other flotsam? And thanks to whom, those godless atheists, those unbelievers the government is hunting down like the plague? You're set to go straight from university to al-Jafr! This girl of yours will be the shame of us.' When I looked toward him, my father was stony-faced. Silently, his heart was breaking; he wouldn't look me in the eye. As if talking to the floor-tiles, he said: 'What they're saying is true, dear girl, it's all for your good.' Et tu Brute!"

[Page from the memoirs of a free officer]

al-Zarqa' military base, 11:30 PM, 13 April 1957

Everything has fallen apart, before we even got started. Our dreams haven't had a chance to trickle down from our minds and into our hands, and it seems like it's already over. Is it true that we are really done?

He must've known about us, I'm sure he did, or else how could've he delivered the pre-emptive but fatal strike?

Right now, we're surrounded, and tomorrow we'll be tried and thrown in jail. The lucky ones who manage to escape by stealing across the border like brigands will forever be exiles.

al-Nabulsi was forced out several days ago, martial law will be proclaimed in a few days, and they're rounding up all the Arab nationalists and the communists. They used us, twice not once: the first time to get rid of Abu Hunayk, when we fell for it and told ourselves that it was our chance to get a seat at the table; and now, to rid the country of Arab nationalists—basically, to rid it of ourselves! Screw this miserable situation.

They say we've encircled Amman, so how come I'm still sitting here with all the roads blocked? The troops of the Alia Brigade crept up on us from Khaww, they burned down the trucks on the road, took over the munitions depots, and surrounded the Officers' Club. I can just hear them chanting: "Down with Abu Nuwwar! Long Live the King!" Yeah, really! If Abu Nuwwar led a coup, hell has frozen over.

We received no orders, no cables, we hadn't even coordinated among ourselves yet. We were just pawns flung across the chessboard, we hadn't matured or ripened yet, we were still cooking... Seven years, and the heat of the forge in our chests has yet to temper the steel in our heads.

What should I be doing, I wonder? I can hear cannon-fire from inside the base and the news from the outside is that large Muslim Brotherhood-led protests, in solidarity with the soldiers besieging us, are at the gates.

I was just told that Maan fled after his troops mutinied, and Ali is on his way back to the palace to await his certain fate; Nadheer and Khalid have reached the Syrian battalion at Mafraq, and I'm stuck here. The deal is done: first they booted us out of the government, and now from the army. A new leaf has been turned.

[The family home, 1979]

What they're saying is true, dear girl, it's all for your good. He couldn't believe that he'd said that. As he stared at the ground, mortified, the procession of familiar ghosts passed before his eyes: those that had stood fast and those that had sold out, and those who had switched their rifles from one shoulder to the other. At the end of the day, he was alone: the banners of the revolution had fallen, and the masses that had revered Abdel Nasser as a saint went to the grave with him. How had it come to this?

He felt too weak to lift his eyes off the floor. He could hear distant voices all around him. And he could also hear the thud of the girl-woman's heart, as if it were his very bones breaking. He was familiar with that sinking feeling, he knew the unhealed psychic wounds it left. He clutched his prostrate head with his fingers, but the breaking went on, random as a feather caught on a gust of wind.

He could see them in his mind's eye, all his old comrades-in-arms: the ambassador, the minister, the director of intelligence. *Director of intelligence—dear God, he went from being a free officer to heading the intelligence department! How could've I been so blind? I wasn't alone, mind you. The Suez Canal was successfully nationalized, land was distributed to the fellahin, the dam was inaugurated, and after Nasser was gone, they witnessed both his killing and theirs; they all hurtled to proclaim the innocence of the sons of Isaac from the blood of Ismail on the altar of the temple, announcing that what belonged to the temple was the temple's, and what belonged to them also belonged to the temple.*

Such a vertiginous fall...and all for nothing. I will bury myself alongside those interred in his grave. We failed, there's no denying it, but maybe with our death something new will arise and go forth. So let me die, let me die now before my time, so that my body becomes the fertile soil for the one that wields the sword after me, let me die. "What they're saying is true, dear girl..." *May you rebel.*

[Books@Café, 2008]

"Two more years, and then I'll follow my dream."

"And what's stopping you from doing it now? You say you're free."

"I *am* free. My father taught me to hold my head high, and to express myself without guile or dissimulation."

"If what you're saying is true, surely you wouldn't depend on my friendship so much. Only with me are you unreservedly you, without airs or protocol, no red carpet to tread on, no ceremony. I accept you as you are. If you were truly free, you could dispense with me."

"Son of a gun! You should feel honored to be sitting here talking to me!"

"That's exactly what I'm saying, and you're confirming it. People who are free are not by their mere presence doing someone a favor or conferring an honor on them. They're there because they're free!"

"You're right. I admit it, I remain bound by my chains, and I've come here to be with you in order to loosen them just for an instant. I am not the same me as the one who lives abroad, I mean: the me who lives over there, some of her is not me. It was much worse before. Do you know what it means to make compromises with someone you don't love? Do you know what happens to a human being when their face is frozen in a fake smile for hours? I would frown for days afterwards just so my face could go back to looking normal. Things are much better now: I go out on my own, I speak my mind, sometimes firing off words like an automatic weapon. I holler and yell, I no longer care, I've become brazen, as they say! But there's still a chain around my feet."

"...."

"Why the silence?"

"I'm thinking. You said you married him to get away, after your family refused to let you study music abroad. And now this too has become an anchor weighing down your runaway ship."

"He wanted to emigrate to the United States. 'This is my opportunity,' I thought. Here, I was bound to the chains of my family; the very air I breathed was heavy. He was my ticket to freedom: I would escape and become myself. Over there, I enrolled in university and played the violin. He didn't object or anything, but when the first baby arrived, followed by the second, the third, and then the fourth, there was no more escaping to be done. And now 29 years later, they too have become another shackle."

"...."

"In two years, the last of the kids will be grown and gone, and I will jump on the first plane back to Amman, to sit with you here, in this very place; and we'll sip on cold Mexican beers, and laugh at the wreckage I left behind. And I'll marry you!"

"Really? You're too much of a coward to do that."

"Oh, if only I had met you 29 years ago..."

"Nah, that's wishful thinking...I wasn't then the man I am now."

"Son of a gun."

••••••

This time wasn't like all the others. She was flying on air as she walked down the boarding ramp to the plane crossing the Atlantic. He would no longer appear in her dreams because he would be there, before her, in the flesh, the real thing. And even though she would continue to collide with a life that she was unsure she had chosen, now she wanted to know—and she made sure she wouldn't be alone.

NOTES:

The Free Officers: a group of officers within the Jordanian army accused of attempting a coup against the monarchy in 1957.

Sleiman al-Nabulsi was the prime minister of Jordan from 29 October 1956 to 10 April 1957. His was the first and last Jordanian cabinet to represent a party that had won a majority of votes in an election. He was forced out of office less than six months after being sworn in as prime minister. Martial law was declared in Jordan shortly afterwards. It lasted until 1989.

Abu Huneyk was a common nickname for John Bagut Glubb, aka Glubb Pasha, the British officer who headed the Jordanian army until early 1956. The moniker was coined because of the mild disfigurement to his lower jaw (*hanak* in Arabic) from a bullet wound.

Khaww is a region in eastern Zarqa where several divisions of the Jordanian army were based.

Ali Abu Nuwwar, the chief-of-staff appointed after the removal of Glubb Pasha in the process of Arabizing the Jordanian army, was blamed for the alleged 1957 coup against the monarchy.

QUANTUM LEAP

The place had changed.

It wasn't in the old city neighborhood anymore. No longer an apartment in a dilapidated building with crumbling walls, where the antiquated fan produced an occasional and feeble breeze as it creaked around collecting dust. No more rusty chairs hardly big enough to sit on, nowhere for dreams to soar.

The place had changed, flown off to a new neighborhood. Instead of one story, now there were two. It had become a villa with a yard in the front and a swimming pool in the back, plus a guardhouse, a red-tile roof, and air conditioning—and a closet for dreams.

• • • • • •

His writer-friends had invited him over. "A gift from the sultan," they'd said, "with no strings attached." So he went.

When he opened the glass door and poked his head in, a blast of cold air tickled the droplets of sweat beading on his forehead. He was struck by the large open space, vacant but for a hanging chair swinging from the ceiling, in which the silhouette of an otherwise invisible person sat holding an electric saw in one hand and a sheaf of papers in the other.

Hanging from butchers' hooks were the headless carcasses of lambs of different sizes. The walls were white but for bright splotches of red.

The silhouette pointed to the newcomer.

"I see landmines in his head," said one carcass.

"I see pencils and pictures and questions," said another.

"I see headless carcasses hanging from butchers' hooks in his head," said the third, as all the carcasses swung to and fro, humming, tails raised, spattering the walls with blood.

The silhouette pointed to the newcomer.

"That one needs a small frame so that his head can look big," said one carcass.

"That head has a golden spoon in its mouth, to make us feel beholden," said another.

"That's the head of a poseur, of a womanizing intellectual," said a third, as all the carcasses swung to and fro, humming, tails raised, spattering the walls with blood.

The silhouette sharpens the electric saw with the sheaf of papers, hitting the pages with the saw, and the red splotches on the walls move around, coalescing and separating: a hammer and sickle appear, no, it's a five-pointed star, or maybe a stylized, arrow-like jeem next to an elongated map...Is it a victory sign? A sun? A peasant? A laborer? Students? The patches of color and the shapes tumble and turn, forming a river that seeps along the corners of the room, through the hallway, and to the back door. The red river spills into the swimming pool.

The silhouette sharpens the electric saw with the sheaf of papers. "Come and get baptized," he says to the head poking through the glass door. "We are the salvation," the carcasses repeat, swinging to and fro, spattering more blood. "Come."

[*Mental whirlwind*]

The pool's slimy water is reddish after the river of blood spills into it. A fire is lit underneath, and servants standing along the edges of the pool stir the liquid with a pole until it turns into a thick sludge, which is then cooled and ladled onto paper plates that were once books. In the evening, the carcasses gather around the pool table to eat the frozen sludge with a dollop of cream and a strawberry.

[What is churning inside the head, poking through the door]

You're just fighting with yourself. From deep in your gut, jagged words erupt, and like the boy who fell from Granddad's balcony, they hurtle down onto the pages of the lexicon, the revolutionary one that the liar carries around and spits on: "Let him have a chair," the sultan says. The chair, a roll of tissue with which to wipe his shit.

Who are you? What are you? A phantom prancing inside an illusory body?

The silence of the slaughtered lambs alone will hold up the sultan's throne.

••••••

There is a large mirror across from the outer door as he is leaving. In the reflection, he can see he looks just the same as when he came in. Behind him, the place gradually transforms into a semblance of the sultan's palace.

He spits on the mirror until his mouth runs dry. "How stupid I was."

He makes a fist and slams it into the glass, and his hand goes right through. He kicks the glass and his foot comes out the other side. He leans his head in, and crosses over. When he turns around, the transformation is complete: there before him is the sultan's palace with its golden doors, its guards, and its surveillance cameras. He looks about, finds a stone and hurls it at the mirrored glass. It shatters. He turns on his heels to make the difficult escape but finds himself in the old neighborhood where children played soccer with a beat-up old ball and laundry hung from the balconies.

He smiles, scratches his head, and goes on his way, slowly. Ever so slowly.

NOTE:

The Arabic letter **jeem** (ج), and the **elongated map with an arrow** make up the logo of the Popular Front for the Liberation of Palestine (PFLP). The *jeem* is the first letter of the group's name in Arabic (jabha); the map is that of Palestine; and the arrow signifies the right of return. The design is commonly believed to be the creation of Palestinian writer and artist Ghassan Kanafani, assassinated by Israel in 1972, but recent reports propose that it was the brainchild of the Palestinian artist Vladimir Tamari (translator's note).

FAYSALI AND WEHDAT

He woke from his green dream. He opened his eyes, which reflected the green of the walls in his green room. He stretched and arched his body, yawning loud enough to shake the foundations and make one's hair stand on end, although no one else was there. He got up and peed, noting how his face, which smelled of cigarettes, was swarthy from unemployment; he scratched his cheeks and chin with its three-day stubble, splashed his face with water that was warm veering on hot (it came straight out of the metal roof-tank that baked in the sun), opened the fridge and drank two glasses of green milk (not his usual single serving), downing them in one gulp, and then started thinking about how to come by the cost of the glass of green milk he would drink the same way on the following day.

He didn't think long. What would happen in a few hours, when the setting sun would be on its descent and that other fire would light up the ground, worried him more. He was thinking about the coming confrontation.

• • • • • •

He woke from his blue dream. He opened his eyes, which reflected the blue of the walls in his blue room. He stretched and arched his body, yawning loud enough to shake the foundations and make one's hair stand on end, although no one else was there. He got up and peed, looked at his face in the mirror and was shocked by his bloodshot eyes, full of small blood vessels and burst capillaries, and the dark puffy bags underneath. He splashed his face with water that was warm veering on hot (it came straight out of the metal roof-tank that baked in the sun), opened the fridge and drank two glasses of blue milk (not his usual single serving), downing them in one gulp, and then started thinking about how to come by the cost of the glass of blue milk he would drink the same way on the following day.

He didn't think long. He too was thinking about the coming confrontation.

• • • • • •

The green man walked through the alleys of the refugee camp, amidst the dusty and swollen faces of malnourished children, and packs of jobless young men. His village west of the river was like a vision in a dream, he'd not once set foot in it, but since his parents and grandparents described it endlessly and in the minutest detail, he knew it house by house, and stone by stone, just like the camp. "That is your homeland and don't you ever forget it," they would say to him, recounting stories of expulsion, massacre, and betrayal—meaning the Arabs' betrayal. "The Arabs betrayed us and never bothered to find out what became of us, and now they torment us, just like the Israelis, if not worse," his father had told him one evening. His friend and the neighbor's son said the same thing.

"Ya wahdana..." had sung the poet of the revolutionary mu'allaqat, deriding the revolution, the umma, the cause, and class war, and ridiculing al-Qawuqji, al-Qassam, Kayed al-Obeidat, Mohammad Hamad al-Hunaiti, and Sultan Ajlouni, as well as the thousands of martyrs, fighters, and militants who came from around and beyond and were immolated in the blaze of the struggle.

Confirming the poet's piercing cry of "ya wahdana," the green man spat on the sea of faces, cursing right and left at all and sundry without distinction.

When he reached the clubhouse, he was lost in a wave of green men streaming forth on their way to the confrontation.

••••••

The blue man walked in the alleys of the neighborhood, with his mind on his humble village over there, to the South or the North. He visited it no more than once or twice a year: going there was hardly ever possible because his moron of a boss drove him like a workhorse and when he got home at night, he was simply exhausted. He looked at the skinny children passing him and at the swarms of jobless young men sprawled out on the sidewalk behind them. "They filched our livelihoods and took over our country's resources," they had told him during closed sessions. "We toil in government and security departments to serve them, basically so that they can enrich themselves and indulge their taste in luxury cars, houses with swimming pools, and educational and employment opportunities. Are we the Red Indians of this country?" The question was a slap in the face.

Which country was that? He had forgotten that his ancestors had come from over there, in the days before colonialism had drawn up borders, in order to escape with their lives and those of their kin. He had forgotten that his very own grandfather had died in the trenches over there after he and his comrades-in-arms had refused the order to withdraw. And that his remains were not found until 60 years later, lying in the garden of one of the houses over there—his grave doused with rose water every day in recognition of the blood oath between them.

"Red Indians." The blue man could attest to it, and he spat on History and its blood-soaked course, piling imprecations on the children of his kind among the residents of the filthy alleys and the dusty-faced people.

When he reached the clubhouse, he was lost in a sea of blue men, and the blue wave streamed out to the confrontation.

[Live broadcast]

The whistle is blown and the two streams launch forward. Chants and anthems fill the air and, at the back, as in a dream, appear the womenfolk of the tribes, ululating: "If you advance, we shall embrace, and spread the cushions. If you retreat, we shall leave, and our parting shall be cold-hearted."

Initially, only tongues skirmish, but soon fists fly, and keffiyehs are raised, for every tribe has its own banner. Leaning in, the two streams charge forward with a roar, and when the whistle blows for the second time, the two sides collide and sparks fly: blades, metal pipes, chains, and soon rivulets of crimson flow. On both sides, the old and the young, including children, hurtle to the ground. Blood mixes with blood, and bodies fall.

Only then (and not before) do the armed men, faces masked, intervene with shields, truncheons, and tear gas grenades. Deploying both gas and truncheons, they form a line separating the two streams and little by little, the blue and green men retreat—one side goes east, the other goes west until all of them disappear from view.

When representatives of the blue men and the green men return to retrieve the bodies, the dead are strewn everywhere. The large guy with a salad bar on his uniform turns the bodies over with his foot, inspecting them. They are colorless, nothing sets them apart but their emaciated, tired, and dusty faces, the faces of people ground down by hunger, misery, oppression, and injustice.

The salad bar man smiles, the thrill of power glimmering in his eyes, as the representatives figure out to which stream the corpses belong.

[New Salvador Dalí painting]

Over there on the hill, in the square fortress that is the upscale neighborhood, the plasma TV with its 52-inch screen is turned off at the press of the remote, and glasses clink as the eight men raise a toast to "enduring."

The one with the twangy English says: Now that was a proper game of origins, just like we trained them to play. Here is my staff, to strike lightning with so that they immolate one other. Such is the way of my world, over which I hold sway from afar.

The one with the seven-branched menorah says: And, here, my spark from your lightning that creeps through the dry wood, lighting the blaze. Such is my land and the obligations arising from the well of ancient books.

His highness and majesty says: Here is my kindling wood, ready for your fire. I will chop and pile and sort, favoring some over others, until they crowd my door. Such is my kingdom in the likeness of a woodshop.

The one whose homeland is lost says: Here is their memory, their blood, and their land. I will level it like a barren plain until nothing is left but wood and fire, and the pierced cloths hoisted above it are the banners of victory and liberation. Such is my kingdom in the likeness of a graveyard.

The one with the medals and stripes says: Here are my arms and here are my legs, with boots and truncheons and metal rods, and here is my brain, like a switch ready to be activated.

The blue-men boss says: Your humble servant, I praise your names day and night; I gather kindling wood in my bag and place it at your door every morning.

The green-men boss says: Your humble servant, I praise your names day and night; I gather kindling wood in my bag and place it at your door every morning.

The owner of the transregional cellphone company says: Here are my pockets, wide open and filled to the brim with the ashes from the fires and the charred remains of the kindling wood. Such is my game.

Voices are raised, the commotion swells, and glasses clink.

••••••

When the green man—panting from all the running and skirmishing—opened the door to his green room, he was surprised to see the blue man panting across the way from him, opening the door to his blue room. The smell of sewage in the street below was oppressive, and the voices of the scrawny-faced children and the idle young men crept up the window.

“Motherfucker.”

“Son of a bitch.”

The blue man hurled a metal pipe at the green man’s head at the very instant the green man spat out a blade that he had kept carefully lodged inside his cheek. The two men fell to the ground as one lifeless corpse.

••••••

Once the putrid smell emanating from the room became unbearable, the neighbors broke down the door. Signs of a violent altercation were everywhere: up-turned tables, broken dishes, and murky blue-green rivulets of coagulated blood trickling down the walls. On the floor was the corpse of one man, with a metal pipe and a blade by his side, his face tenebrous and powdery, his skull split open, with a viscous incised wound running from the side of his nose to the outer edge of his right eye.

NOTES:

Ya wahdana ("O how alone we are") is the cry uttered by the Palestinian poet Mahmoud Darwish in his long poem "Madeeh al-Thull al-'Aali," which references the abandonment of the Palestinians to their desperate fate during the Israeli siege of Beirut in 1982.

al-Qawuqji, al-Qassam, Kayed al-Obeidat, Mohammad Hamad al-Hunaiti, and Sultan Ajlouni: Since the colonization of Palestine was considered an invasion of the entire region and its peoples, freedom fighters from the Arab world and beyond (like those whose names are mentioned here, hailing from what is now Syria and Jordan) contributed to, and sometimes led, the struggle against British and Zionist colonization in Palestine.

"If you advance, we shall embrace . . ." are verses attributed to Hind Bint Utbah, uttered when she and the women of Qureish accompanied the Meccan forces into the battle of Uhud. The women drummed on their dafs to urge their warriors on against the forces of Medina led by Muhammad.

AUTHOR'S NOTE FOR THE CONTEXTULIZATION OF THE STORY:

In Jordan, a deep fault line running through society pertains to the geographical origin of citizens relative to the River Jordan: those of East Bank lineage ("Jordanian Jordanians") versus those of West Bank lineage ("Palestinian Jordanians"). Notwithstanding its superficial discourse to the contrary, the regime maintains the functioning of this cleavage in subtle ways, normalizing a corrupt and oppressive ruling class, which it uses as both a buffer and mediator. The management of this cleavage is a textbook example of the ways in which authoritarianism manipulates bigotry and nurtures fascist tendencies for its own survival.

Nowhere does this fault line acquire fuller expression than in the Jordanian premier soccer league. al-Faisaly and Wehdat are the league's two main clubs and traditional rivals. The former (with its distinctive blue jerseys) draws its fan-base and supporters from among Jordanian Jordanians; the latter (with its distinctive green jerseys), hailing from Amman's eponymous Palestinian refugee camp, is the team of Palestinian Jordanians. The rival sides commonly chant racist epithets and profanities throughout the matches, sometimes directing them against the regime. Although criticism of the monarchy constitutes a red line in Jordan, it is tolerated in that setting.

The story also explores postcolonial identities. The maps (and thus the subsequent identities) of the polities we know as Jordan, Palestine, Lebanon, and Syria were drawn by the ruling colonial powers—the French and the British—following the end of World War I and the collapse of the Ottoman Empire. Neo-colonialism and interventionism are still alive and well in the region, as evidenced by the disproportionate influence of the United States in Jordanian politics (with Jordan considered a "close ally of the US"), and the 1948 establishment in Palestine of the settler-colonial state known as Israel. Despite widespread poverty and corruption, as well as the extreme concentration of power, lack of popular democracy, and absence of true sovereignty in Jordan, global, regional, and local actors are able to maintain the status quo partly by feeding this rupture.

STARDUST

I'm tired of turning the dials of History. There is nothing there but the motion of mouths opening and closing as an anesthetizing saccharine solution is dropped into them. I look at them: they are motionless and shackled, sap sucked dry, faces covered in imbecilic smiles. Who are these people all around me? Do I know them? Why are they here? Why am I here? Where have they gone? Where did the picture go? Where am I? What. Is. Happening? There's...cz-cz-cz-cz-cz-sh-sh-sh-sh-sh-sh...

[First answer]

The second law of thermodynamics: Physical systems tend toward change from being highly ordered to more disordered formations. The entropy of an isolated system that is not in equilibrium tends to increase over time. The entropy of the universe tends to a maximum.

• • • • • •

"Why am I here, in the midst of all this destruction?" was the question running through his mind when he glimpsed dark gray clouds threatening overhead. People looked at him strangely as he yelled at the top of his lungs, "They're just the fallout from a massive nuclear explosion."

"Crazy guy," someone said, hurrying past.

"You idiots, sneaking your way through air that is polluted with car exhaust, and all that hookah and cigarette smoke. Look at the bare ground between the concrete mounds: the soil is red. Red soil, do you hear? Soil that is fertile and that you are paving with asphalt and concrete, and mounds of stone so that you can facilitate the flow of your garbage and the dissemination of your abominable noise."

The only person that dared approach him was a beggar child, his nostrils crusty with dry snot. "Sir, you got a smoke for me?"

"You're knee high to a flea," the man responded, gesturing with his index and thumb stacked on top of one another, "and you smoke? Why don't you wait a while, until you've grown taller and more foolish?"

[Second answer]

"Human beings define their reality through suffering and misery. The perfect world was a dream that your primitive cerebrum kept trying to wake up from. I'd like to share a revelation that I've had during my time here. It came to me when I tried to classify your species and I realized that you're not actually mammals. Every mammal on this planet instinctively develops a natural equilibrium with the surrounding environment but you humans do not. You move to an area and you multiply and multiply, until every natural resource is consumed and the only way you can survive is to spread to another area. There is another organism on this planet that follows the same pattern. Do you know what it is? A virus. Human beings are a disease, a cancer of this planet. You're a plague."

••••••

"Viruses." When the sound of that voice hit her ear, the young woman stumbled and almost fell over, dropping her cellphone to the ground. "Over the course of tens of thousands of years, viruses have invaded us and their genes have co-mingled with ours. We have become like them, only worse. Extinction—mass extinction—awaits."

He went on his way, thundering past her and kicking a young man about to climb into a four-wheel drive. "We will all be extinct, you fool," he exclaimed as he turned toward the passers-by who had begun to gather around.

"Dear biped fossils, you think you are intelligent creatures? What kind of intelligence has evolved in you that you are addicted to petroleum, uranium, and electromagnetic waves? They say that intelligence is the property of highly complex matter. What complexity is it that you boast about when you sleep in your own radioactive shit? Maybe if we went back to being unintelligent matter we would avert the bloodbaths, the mountains of garbage, the huge and viscous maritime oil spills. Everyone wants a happy ending. Here's a happy ending for you: may you all become extinct."

••••••

He remembered a woman who not long ago had been his wife. She wanted to have a baby.

"Aren't there enough wretched people on Earth?" he'd tell her. She'd get upset and start crying. And then, she'd go and complain to his mother.

"Don't you want someone to carry on the family name after you, my son? Do you want all trace of you to disappear?"

My name? It is with my nails that I will engrave my name on the face of this wretched history. I would change its course by even a fraction of a degree if I could. Would that I could dissolve and be soaked up by the flowers planted in the soil over my grave. A son would immortalize me, you say? Ah, the wretchedness of the selfish gene! Let him save himself, if he can! Who am I to make decisions for him? What kind of free being is it whose existence is brought about by someone else? No, that can't be right. How would I know whether he wanted to exist in the first place? Shall I say, "Be!" that he might come into existence at my command and in spite of himself so that I enjoy being a mini-God? This planet doesn't need any more people. Don't you worry; the species is safe and sound. We're going to be the death of the planet before we're done dying.

[Third answer]

"Who am I? Who are you? Who are we?" he was screaming now.

Carl Sagan's voice rang out. "We are nothing but a handful of stardust."

••••••

Sirens sounded. Police cars arrived, more bystanders gathered around. A man lay on the ground shouting, "Destruction. Red soil. Viruses. Stars. We will be extinct, you fools."

Two policemen overpowered him and dragged him off, kicking and screaming.

“Just a crazy man,” a woman told her neighbor looking out of her apartment window.

The police sirens subsided and disappeared into the distance. She drew the curtains closed.

•••••••

Before closing his eyes for the last time, he felt a warm liquid seeping from the tip of his nose; his tongue, between his front teeth, felt what seemed to be a small window, while his wrists, handcuffed behind his back, felt as if they were going to explode.

One of his eyes was swollen, he couldn’t fully open the eyelid, but the other eye was fine. He could see the policemen whispering behind the bars in front of him. He figured they were talking about him because there was no one else in the lock-up. Soon afterwards, there was the awful sound of metal scraping against metal and slamming: the door opened. Two men in white coats appeared. Why were they here?

When he saw the large syringe one of them was holding, he understood. The stabbing of his buttock and the pressure of the injected liquid were the last things he sensed before passing out, his indignant cry silenced.

[Fourth answer]

"Oh, what a beautiful place!"

He turned toward the sunlight glinting off the glass high-rises. His eyes followed a large black car. The smell of grilling titillated his nostrils and his hormones erupted when a young woman winked at him. The large digital advertising screens kept flipping overhead: *You deserve more; It isn't rocket science: Increase your investment and grow your profit; We can make your dreams come true: live the American dream right here; Only three days left for you to win the JD 250,000; We'll build your dream with this housing loan; Opportunity doesn't knock twice: own your dream car now; It's your world alone: enjoy it with our special offers.*

HERE. A light glimmered ahead and his excitement rose as he set off toward it. He noticed the people around him for the first time, and they were all walking in the same direction. He quickened his pace, broke into a run, but felt he was running in place. When he looked at the others, he noticed that the distance between them remained unchanged.

For a moment, he almost thought he should stop but just then, as if about to collide with his head, **HERE** lit up again in front of him. It went off but he was sure it was closer. He spurred himself on. He licked his upper lip with his tongue and bit down on his lower one, the sweat beading on his forehead. He wiped off the droplets trickling into his eyes with his shirtsleeve. He could feel himself getting hotter and his heart beating furiously:

apartment, car, cellphone, sexy girl, shiny glass buildings... threshold to **HERE.**

It all looked so close but he didn't seem to be making any headway. Looking at one another, the others hurried on past, quickening their pace.

••••••

It was a dark, cold, and damp space. The air was heavy with the breath of so many others. He couldn't tell how many. Hundreds? Thousands? Millions? Billions? Gazing into the distance, everything looked blurred, and the harder he tried, the more spots there were...black ones, white ones, and gray ones, accompanied by the dull, buzzing noise: cz cz cz cz cz cz cz cz sh sh sh...

Looking in front of him, he can see the sewing machine and the pieces of fabric quite clearly, his hands catching hold of the fabric in an involuntary, reflex gesture, and running it under the needles bobbing up and down, turning it into shirts. On the tag, he can make out the name of the famous international brand, and the words "Made in QIZ-Jordan" written underneath.

Looking in front of him, he can hear talking, but can't understand what's being said—just the way it was when actors spoke in those Indian movies he watched as a teenager. He didn't understand a word and there were no subtitles. He listened and listened, but he still couldn't understand. The large hall was dark, cold and damp, its air thick, so thick, with everything in the distance looking blurred.

For a second, he entertains the thought of stopping. "Focus on what's in front of you," booms a voice from overhead speakers. "To make progress, you must mind your own business."

"Yes, that's right, there's no one else but me here," he murmurs under his breath. "It's just me, and hell is other people," he tells her. "I..." he's shouting at her now, weaving between the glass buildings, the luxury cars, and the woman who had winked at him. He stretches out his hand, he can almost touch her, he quickens his pace; for an instant it appears that he's not making any headway, so he runs even faster, dripping with perspiration.

[Fifth and last answer]

Amidst the clamor of women and children, like static in the background, the voice of Jim Jones rises up loud and clear: "To me death is not a fearful thing. It's living that's cursed. We didn't commit suicide. We committed an act of revolutionary suicide protesting the conditions of an inhumane world."

NOTES:

Second Answer: the text that follows this heading is a rearranged passage of dialogue from *The Matrix*, a film by the Wachowski Sisters.

QIZ stands for Qualified Industrial Zones, tax-free industrial zones established in Jordan under the U.S.-Israeli free trade agreement drawn up in the wake of the so-called peace treaty between the Jordanian and Israeli governments in 1994. Goods manufactured in such zones are permitted to enter American markets free of duty so long as at least 8% of their value added originates in Israel. The overwhelming majority of Jordanian QIZs are textile manufacturing facilities where over half the workers are not Jordanians but contracted guest workers from South Asia and China who often pay lump sums of several thousand dollars to get hired by a garment factory. Working conditions are notoriously bad and wages pitifully low. Egypt later followed the Jordanian example.

INTELLECTUALS

[One]

Angry jabs and tensed forearms filter through the words, his pencil stabs, searing the paper, red flags fluttering between the lines, alongside images of Nasser, Chavez, Hassan Nasrallah, and Che Guevara. People cower under the tables invoking God's mercy as he heaps Judgment Day curses on the regime, its apologists and loyalists, hands out affidavits of innocence, or guilt, to comrades, and issues his manifesto of nationalism-unity-resistance-internationalism against the backdrop of Kalashnikov fire.

But when he leaves his desk, and steps away from the newspaper financed by a sectarian foundation that pays his salary, he makes his way to the cubicle of a low-level civil servant and petitions for political and financial assistance to the revolutionary forum he heads. At the end of the night, he meets up with old friends, born-again from the past with the touch of Judas Iscariot. "I am the resurrection and the life: he that believeth in me, though he were dead, yet shall he live. Come forth," he commanded, and despite the voice that had cried from afar—*they stink, for they have been dead four decades*—they had all risen: the loyalist and the neo-liberal, the right-winger and the fundamentalist, the chauvinist and the opportunist.

Here then were his disciples, their hands and feet bound in linen strips, their faces wrapped in cloth, and after he had loosened their binds and let them go, they set about plotting to overthrow nationalism-internationalism-resistance-revolution, and everything else that was not them.

[Two]

Ever since letting his hair and beard grow out, he had known—without the shadow of a doubt—that he was at least one part artist, and he lived the role fully. He left his family home, rented a dingy room, and filled it with feral cats and cigarette ends. He fasted to the point that he wouldn't stir up so much as a wisp of air when walking by, and once he was done filling his computer, sketch pad, or fabric (it made no difference which) with his scribbles, he went onto other art forms, notably photography, film directing, and petty conspiracies. "It's all art," he would say, "and the artist must experiment, struggle, and experience birth pangs to achieve breakthroughs and transformation."

And that is how, in the span of seven days, our friend went from left to right to center without a day of rest: he discovered foreign aid and diplomatic support; he explored conformity and non-conformity; he experienced passing pangs of conscience and transient feelings of isolation; he fought one battle after another, and continued laboring since the artist's travails were, in his view, endless.

His problem was women. He had yet to deflower a single one, but a true artist, as everyone knows, must exert a magnetic attraction for the opposite sex. His authenticity therefore remained in question: the goddesses were angry and the baptismal font stood dry, its waters sequestered in their anger.

It wasn't long, however, before his (just-as-intellectual) female friends unmasked him and one of them took to baring parts of her tender flesh to him, which he licked and sniffed before setting off, his tail wagging, to bark at whomever lay at the end of the imaginary line extending from her commanding, and desired, finger.

At the end of the day, after reaping his share of sticks and stones and kicks, he would come back to find the door (from which she had sent him off) closed. His head pummeled by the unmistakable sound of amorous voices inside, he'd gather himself and return to the dingy room filled with feral cats and cigarette ends, curl up in a fetal position, and not sleep.

[Three]

When she discovered her intellectual of a husband in her bed, plunged deep between the legs of another woman (also an intellectual), she exclaimed loud enough for everyone to hear that she'd stuff her shoes in his mouth. There was little he could do but jump up stark naked, throw himself at her feet, and snatch one of her shoes. "Here it is, in my mouth! What else? Up my ass, too!" he exclaimed, standing up to open all the windows, still biting down on her footwear.

When the play ended, in which she was the sole protagonist, she really began to believe that there were no other heroines, but after the director got all the accolades, her whole world crumbled. How could a monodrama have two heroines? She ranted and raved until they threw her out—just like the shoes hanging from her husband's mouth and out of his backside—and the play went on with another actress.

Those two events were more than she could bear, and she sank into a dank and solitary cell, an abyss, of despair.

Since she couldn't stand anything but herself and she couldn't bear the solitude—she just had to be with people, if only one other person—she fell apart, went to pieces; and then turned to film directing. Films, after all, were the fiefdoms of absolute despots who received sole attribution. Her name alone would glimmer, with no partner sharing the limelight: "A film by..." In her pre-Copernican vision, where Earth lay at the center of the universe, she, as the center of the world, would become the center of the center. Gyrating at breakneck speed, the center shatters, and the pieces fly in every direction.

Every direction imaginable: so that there was no harm, for instance, in obtaining a visa from the Israeli embassy in Amman and, after the winds of change began to blow, in protesting at its doors, demanding that it be shut down and for its presence to be erased. Nor was it a problem if she protested the U.S. occupation of Iraq and simultaneously used the occupier's funds to take part in the International Visitor Program to get to know "the enemy's culture." And it also wasn't an issue to defend independent art but get her production costs paid in dollars reaped from the irrigation ditches of the land of the two rivers. Whole as it was, the self was eminently capable of encompassing all things, including contradiction.

Inspired by her husband, the subjugation of men became a driving obsession, in life as well as art. She rode them roughshod after flinging herself at them, and woe betide those who rejected her advances. At them, she directed a stream of invective and obscenities, like garbage hurled from a bucket. She was free to fuck with them but they were not free to refuse her. It was at this point that all the aforementioned contradictions resolved, fusing together with the sharpness of a knife that she threw haphazardly, only to find herself once more swimming in that vast and limitless bucket of filth that had no perimeter, circumference, or rim.

Are you enjoying yourself yet? Yes, *you*, dear reader. Don't be incredulous: in a nightmare, she might open the bathroom door while you stand naked under the hot stream of the shower. She might insinuate her fingers into your fly while you're driving. She might throw herself at you, legs wide open, and panting with the excitement of a woman who's gone too long without being laid. But when she does, and then quenches her thirst (or not), she will feel that shoe obstructing her breathing, and her tawdriness worming its way into her, devouring her flesh bit by bit. There must have been a criminal, some scumbag who had driven or forced her, exploited her feelings, and trifled with her innocence. And that scumbag is you: yes, you, who are reading this and enjoying the vision of her imagined flesh. Yes, *you*, motherfucker.

No, we're not done yet, there's still a ways to go until she reaches her solipsistic climax. Once the desired men who don't reciprocate her feelings penetrate her in her dream, she snaps their cocks between her thighs, thrusts into herself head first and coils herself up tightly to become the center of the vortex, spinning faster and faster, its pieces flying in every direction as it breaks up and disintegrates.

[In the kitchen of the Almighty Leader]

The well-trained servant comes in every day and opens the fridge, taking a specimen from [*One*], another from [*Two*], and a third from [*Three*]. He drops them into the blender, runs the machine at maximum speed, and pours the thick liquid into a tall glass for the Almighty Leader to drink first thing in the morning—in accordance with the palace physician's instructions—in order to enjoy life everlasting.

SOLITUDE

To Ayed Nab'a

The stone masonry wall is damp and covered in a musty film of mold. There is a faint, fetid smell. Colored lights rotate continuously, and there are faraway-but-close sounds of car tires, cheap music, and indistinguishable conversation.

They sit side by side on the sofa, his hand in hers. Skinny and bushy-haired, their drooping eyelids are swollen. They've been sitting here, in hibernation mode, for a very long time, covered by a thick coating of dust. In the crannies of their immobile bodies, spiders have woven webs that no breeze disturbs.

Their chests rise and fall and the quiet sound of their inhalations alone belie the certainty that they are dead. There is not even the flutter of an eyelid: their eyes, permanently open, are fixed on the opposite wall.

All the walls are bare except for the one with the liquid crystal display TV flashing ever-changing pictures: a dubbed Turkish series, nude women cavorting to the tune of some vulgar melody; the Oprah Winfrey show; commercials advertising cooking oil, feminine pads, and a mobile phone; *Who's A Millionaire*, a news program whose two relaxed anchors shake their heads in a deliberate show of gravitas; *Star Academy*; and a Hollywood action film being replayed for the nth time with the obligatory car chases, guns, and "fuck" translated as "damn." The colors flicker endlessly, mirrored in their sallow eyes.

Complete obscurity abruptly descends following the crackle of an electric short circuit overhead. Before the screen dies, the flickering colored images are momentarily distorted, and as the last one briefly fixes onto their eyes, total darkness envelops the room.

The silence is brief.

"Hey. Get up and open the window," she says.

"How would I know to do that? I've been sitting on this sofa like you ever since I've known I was sitting on the sofa watching the window. I only know what you know, we've watched it all from this window together. I don't know how to open or close it, and we've never closed the window—it's always been open. Shouldn't I know how to close it in order to know how to open it?"

"Didn't you hear what I said, dammit? Get up and open the window," she says.

"I've learned so many things from the window. I've seen magical worlds and beautiful women, god-humans and machine-humans, massacres and defeats, victories and broken hearts. And sex, oh the sex! Did you see how that girl in the commercial was humping the chocolate bar? Now that's what I call a commercial! But the window didn't teach me how to close or open it. It's always been open. Don't you think that's strange?"

"I'm tired of your excuses, you loser. Don't you understand that we will suffocate and die with the window closed? I'm suffocating right now. Suffocating," she says.

"Well, why don't we try seeing what it's like to have the window closed just this once? That's exactly what I'm thinking right now and, to be more precise, I'm wondering why we didn't try and extend our arms and heads from the window? Why didn't we call out to one of those people sitting outside or passing by? I could've asked one of those women humping on the sofa for a bar of chocolate. I could've joined the protest at 10 Downing Street. I could've invited that singer to sit with us. Some singer she was! The only thing you could hear was the sound of all that silicone! I could've helped the emergency medics with that kid who was riddled with shrapnel holes. What was he screaming? I don't remember anymore. But we remained silent, just watching. I should've poked my head out of the window."

"Ohhhh, I'm suffocating here. You asshole, just open the window. You're jailing me here, killing me." She was screaming by now, and her screams grew louder and louder until they disappeared up the big opening in the ceiling, reverberated through the large pipes, and then the smaller ones, smaller, and smaller, and smaller...

••••••

The glass almost broke after slipping from between the housewife's soapy fingers as she heard a voice coming up through the sink. "Ohhhh, I'm suffocating here. Open the window." In his brand new suit and with a laptop in his briefcase, the twenty-something man recently hired by a large financial company lost his footing and almost tripped over the voice coming up the manhole, "You asshole. You're jailing me here, killing me. Open the window." And the old man who had popped a Viagra pill and was lathering up with scented soap under the hot shower almost slipped over the voice rising up between his feet, "You're killing me. Open the window."

••••••

"Hello, 911? Yes, hello. There's a voice coming up the sink drain. Yes, yes. Incomprehensible words, something about a closed window...OK. You're going to take care of it? Thank you very much."

"Hello, 911? Yes. I was walking in the street and I heard strange voices inside the manhole...Something about suffocation and death and a window...OK, I knew you'd look into it. Have a good day."

"Hello...I want to report something that happened earlier today. There were strange voices coming up the drain in the shower. A window, and jail, and things I didn't understand. You say there are other similar reports? It's not just me hearing those things? And you're addressing the problem? Oh, OK! You sure move fast. Bye."

• • • • • •

In the midst of the large valley in the city of hills, the bodies of exhausted foreign workers shuddered as they bore down on the pneumatic drills rebounding against the pressure of their arms. Nearby, a large yellow earth-digger drove its huge metal boring-post into the ground, and bulldozers cleared the accumulated debris.

The crater was ten meters deep, and the crew sent out by the authorities used special ropes to scale down to the bottom. From there, they followed the city's massive sewers.

"Drop the hose," one of them said, speaking into a microphone dangling in front of his mouth, as two others examined a tangled mass of wires. An ear-splitting scream came out of the large opening to the side: "Open the window, you loser...I'm suffocating...I'm going to die."

Four of the crewmen fixed wooden planks over the opening and crisscrossed them with metal rods. No sooner had the two guys with the wires called out, "Ready now, sir," than the screaming from below stopped. The faraway-but-close sounds of car tires, cheap music, and indistinguishable conversation rushed in as faint and flickering colored lights filtered through the wooden planks and the metal rods.

"Start pumping," said the dangling microphone guy, and everything was drowned in liquid concrete.

PAPER ON TABLE NEXT TO OVERTURNED CHAIR

February 9, 2008

I haven't yet tried true exile, the kind that takes you far from familiar places and known people. I imagine that it's no worse a predicament than the one I'm in already because I can't think of anything harder than feeling alienated among the intimate strangers of my daily life. When I look in their faces, I see nothing but blank pages, unmarked but for the number at the bottom, like the dates on a calendar, one blank page-day identical to the next except for that number.

Why am I supposed to celebrate such a life?

What a stupid question. For the few years since becoming woke, I've been certain of two things: the freedom of human beings and their responsibility for their actions. I find it ridiculous when people blame others for their shortcomings, like when someone says, Oh man, it's your fault I got angry. And I can't but laugh in the face of those always cussing others out for their own flaws—Goddamn so-and-so who made me forget (or fight, or kill, or...)—as though by faulting others they're off the hook—so that they're mere innocents, wretches, or ignoramuses. Victims led by destiny and fate to the inevitability of the Preserved Tablet, the divine decree: it was meant to be, it was written.

Now, after all that's happened, I acknowledge that we are condemned to life; I have to recognize that not only are we not free in choosing freedom, as some existentialists would have us believe—even though I've always thought that was an oxymoron—but we are also not free in that we have no choice in the matter of being born.

"This is what my father inflicted upon me."

But still, I ask: has my life made a difference? Will my death? Am I any more significant than an insect? Does an insect not make a difference? What about its death? I don't know. Life will dissipate, and these questions will no doubt remain unanswered.

I wonder what was going on in Tayseer al-Sboul's head when he pressed the trigger? Or what mythical courage inhabited Khalil Hawi when he blew his head open on the balcony of his Beirut apartment? Were these acts of ultimate self-denial? Were they the epitome of courage, or the height of cowardice?

There were five of us in the group: three guys and two girls. When asked to prick our fingers with a pin in order to determine our blood group at the university biology lab, not one of us had the courage to do it: each of us pricked the other's. How then can human beings—who are afraid of the tiniest pinprick—mete out self-punishment that is irreversible? That has to be courage.

Or resignation.

What kind of cowardice would drive such extraordinary, albeit rare, individuals (whether at the threshold of a talented life or at the height of their gifts) to bail out in this awful way? Is there not also some shortfall involved in their inability to successfully resolve whatever crisis they were facing?

People say that our mental and cognitive capabilities are critically heightened when facing really tough times, so how is it that the suicide-in-the-making was unable to overcome his predicament when deeply immersed in the kind of circumstances that pertain most keenly to thinking and the mind? Where then was Pavlov? Had Tayseer not heard of Pavlov and his dogs, or of positive reinforcement?

And yet:

Are we supposed to turn into salivating dogs every time we hear a bell or the footsteps of the guards approaching? Are we supposed to find a solution to every problem, like a scientist expects to in accordance with his experiments? The harder it is, the easier it gets... Just that mechanically? Not likely.

Personally, I refuse to become a Pavlovian dog.

I refuse to even salivate. I'll destroy the bell and bite the foot of that saliva-addicted scientist. I have a right to draw outside the lines, to scream, to cry, and to cackle with laughter. And also, to cuss and blaspheme. And to die.

The other world. That unknown.

I often feel an urge to know what happens after death. But it appears that the only path to such knowledge is... death itself.

I'm the logical product of human history. Ever since the dawn of consciousness, we have been asking the same unanswered question, because it's a one-way street. Now I want to know, and I want to go down that road. What's here for me anyway?

Let me make a list: wars, massacres, plagues, rape, lies, thievery, deception, oppression, torture, exile, hypocrisy, sickness, hunger, racism, military coups, pollution, and on, and on.

You might retort: science, love, music, art, poetry. OK, then: is all the poetry in the world worth the life of an African child who has starved to death when the earth is producing many times the amount of food necessary to human survival? Is all the love in the world capable of making up for the damage inflicted on a girl who has been gang-raped by blond soldiers that crossed the oceans for "Iraqi freedom?"

What is tragi-comical, if not downright disgraceful, is that the species that has wreaked such terrible devastation continues to exist and to "progress" inexorably, while a huge number of species and organisms—many of them more powerful and far grander—have become extinct. And the waitlist is long.

Humankind's response? Inhabit the earth, we were commanded! Funny...Not!

As for me, Frayj—

a stupid marginal that's never written anything for the sake of it other than these lines—I declare my rebellion against it all. From A to Z. My poor, limited, brain can't stand anymore of this. It can't tolerate the Qana massacre or the shelling of the 'Amiriyyah shelter; not the Hiroshima bomb, or Agent Orange; not the ruling party's power grab or what is happening in the jails of the Mukhabarat. And not my father, or hers.

I may not marry her: I'm Christian and she's Muslim.

Religion: Christian. That's what it says on the back of my ID card. Even though I don't believe in God, I am branded just like the slaughtered calves at the municipal slaughterhouse. All of us are, from the day we are born. No sooner do we draw our first breath and utter that first cry than we smell the odor of seared flesh—the branding is done not only with ink but with fire. The skinned calves have it better: ink is used to brand them, and only after they are dead, not before they see the light of day.

From the moment of emergence as a member of Homo sapiens, we become: Black, Sunni, Jordanian, Catholic, Asian, Indian, Palestinian, Shi'i, Kurdish, Greek-Orthodox, Arab, Turkish, White, Red, Amazigh. And when one of us is a combination of these, the effect of the branding is just multiplied.

To the slaughterhouse?

Never. I will rebel against it, against them. Against all those trying to turn us into carbon copies of themselves. Against all those trying to feed us through the assembly line, and stamping a serial number on our backsides so that they can complete the annual inventory. And I will rebel against myself too. Why not? Who says I don't oppress myself? Who says I'm not sitting inside some paradigm fashioned by someone else, or by me, in order to accommodate others?

Yes, I will step out.

When you read these lines, I will have begun my first real adventure toward the unknown, without branding seals, or IDs, or skin color. Going forward, nothing will convince me to submit. I simply won't be here. My new friend, the angel of death 'Izra'il and I will be more than halfway there. I leave to you "your" Earth and your "lives" to spread corruption as you see fit.

As for me, I'm tired of all this.

NOTES:

"This is what my father inflicted upon me" is attributed to Abul 'Alaa' al-Maari, the blind 10th century poet, philosopher, and writer, known for being a skeptic and freethinker who invoked reason as the only real source of truth. It is said that he wanted his epitaph to state that his life had been a wrong done by his father and not by himself. (Translator's note.)

Tayseer al-Sboul (1939-73) was a Jordanian poet and writer who committed suicide in the flower of youth. His most significant work is a novel entitled *You as of Today*.

Khalil Hawi (1919-82) was a prominent Lebanese poet who killed himself two days after the beginning of the 1982 Israeli invasion of Lebanon.

In Jordan, and other countries, government regulations require slaughtered animals to be skinned and **branded** with an **ink** stamp at the abattoir. (Translator's note.)

GAZA

ETCHED IN RED

Israel is pounding Gaza. Dozens of corpses lie strewn on the ground. One of them mumbles something. When you approach, you hear: ash-hadu anna la ilaha illa-laah...

Nearing final immolation, the corpse chants the death song: blood/rain, blood/rain, blood/rain.

• • • • • • •

His strides long, Death stalks the land. He counts off, "One... twenty...three hundred...four thousand...five million...six billion..." requisitioning each and every one of Earth's inhabitants. "You all are mine."

Death smiles as his devoted children play with some of his favorite toys: Apache helicopters; F-16s; and *boom* goes another rocket. On the screen, the plume of smoke billows up in the distance, and indigo bodies lie scattered around the asphalt underneath—a hand here, a leg there, and over here, a jaw: la-ilah-illa-laah...I bear witness that there is no god but God.

••••••

He's sitting up, trunk swaying, glassy eyes rolling in their sockets. The fire rages nearby but he can't see a thing. He can only feel the gushing liquid, the rivulets of blood running down his face.

••••••

"Allahu akbar." The chant explodes as an EMT cuts through the crowd holding aloft a child, his body eviscerated by a rocket.

••••••

A mass of corpses-to-be carry corpses-that-are, going to their inexorable fate: the fireball spawned by the F-16's assault of the sky.

••••••

Walking home from school feeling elated, a young girl reclines under the luxuriant foliage of an olive tree felled by a random rocket. "How beautiful you are," her sweetheart had whispered surreptitiously, pressing a rose into her hand. The rose is red. Blood red, the color of her happy, smiling face.

••••••

Seventy corpses on the road. One for every kilometer between Jerusalem and Amman. The Israeli flag flutters proudly over the hills east of the Jordan. The West Bank is ours, it brags. And the East Bank too.

Three hundred and forty-seven bodies on the road. One for each kilometer between Gaza and Cairo. The Israeli flag flutters proudly over a building by the Nile. From the Nile to the Euphrates, it brags, lies the Land of Israel.

••••••

The sea is calm. Below the surface, shoals of fish glide among the multi-colored coral. Above, the metal-gray warship fires its load on bands of children, leaving them swimming in water the color of blood.

••••••

The crossing points are closed off so that bread can't be shipped in, but today they will be wide open to welcome those that have died.

ETCHED IN WHITE

Israel visits him in his dream: silently, the massive wall rises sky-high before his eyes.

••••••

The blue sky is streaked with the F-16's white trails and birds scatter from the rush of warm air produced by the rotors of the Apache helicopters.

Mere seconds pass, and the boom is heard. The earth trembles. It isn't God's voice addressing Moses, nor is it the sound of the stone tablets crashing down in the desert. "Thou shalt not kill," enjoin the Ten Commandments, but the missile brings down the entire building, propelled by Yahweh's resolve at the speed of David's slingshot. The head of a girl struggles to poke through the fine white dust: the bodies of her thirteen siblings are buried deep in the rubble, clutching at what remains of their mother.

A thick white cloud blankets the ground. It rolls under the doors, seeping through the window frames and the pock-marked walls—the fog produced by the shell is so thick that nothing is visible; everywhere, sounds of coughing and gasping for air amid the metallic smell. A meteor shower of white phosphorus cascades down in bursts, setting the air ablaze. People run helter-skelter, bits of charred flesh spilling to the ground.

The generals rejoice at the firework display.

••••••

Walking through Hayy al-Zeytoun, his eyes fix on the prostrate skeletons. He brushes away the haze of misery and continues on. He walks far, far away...

Far away to the Southeast: *Luxurious Flat in Victory City, on the Gulf's Waterfront: Move in Now!* He opens the door and enters. Here in the peninsula, sounds are different. Although white trails also streak the sky, birds do not scatter.

Under the wing, the star-spangled banner shimmers for an instant before USAF appears in fluorescent letters.

He jumps from the window and lands among the dense date palm groves and wetlands that line the banks of the two rivers. Soldiers bristling with M-16s advance in single file, fingers on triggers. They pass by him as if he has no more substance than the wisp of a breeze. A rooster crows, chickens cluck, there is the hee-haw of a donkey, and then the burst of a flamethrower, which turns the village into a ball of fire, a miniature sun.

• • • • • •

When he woke up from the nightmare, there were empty bullet casings, as well as traces of blood and soot, scattered across the room and all over his bed covers. From the large hole in the ceiling, he could see the blue sky, streaked with white trails. But no birds. An unexploded rocket had pierced his abdomen.

To his right, sat Israel with these comforting words: "We are pained by every single civilian death; we do not target women and children; we only kill terrorists; we will launch an investigation into what happened here."

He smiled, looked up at the blue sky again and watched it slowly turn crimson. A flock of birds flew by overhead. Balloons and paper planes, too. He wrapped the explosive belt tight around his middle, and squeezed on the detonator.

CROSSING

To Ra'ed Abdel-Haq

1—First Attempt

You cross the bridge suspended over the canal. Colored ships slowly glide across the surface of blue waters below. Now and then, from beyond the hills of fine sand, a date palm emerges, a village, some people. Fish dart across the lake and a swarthy, dusty child poses for the camera, stick in hand.

••••••

Eight people on their way to Gaza: the road is long and strewn with checkpoints.

"Salamu alaikum," and we go through the second checkpoint; at the third, nobody's there. And at the fourth, a policeman waves us on. Just like that.

The sun is warm and everything is coming together, it seems. Yesterday, rumor had it that the crossing would be open between 10 AM and 4 PM. It was only a rumor, but oh, the hope that tickled their minds: They would get through.

••••••

Old, beat-up buses and cars stood under the dilapidated bridge. The green Mercedes whisked them off before they could reach the bus, and now they were lurching through the chaos of Cairo traffic.

Ayed would not desist. Tracking them from the front, from the back, from above, from below, as they try to dodge the large lens of his camera. The pressure gets under their skin, making them tense and uneasy: Who likes being under constant surveillance?

In the backseat is the guy with the explosive name: Nasrallah, God's victory. The very antithesis of nasr Allah—but like his paintings, he's as calm as a puff of clouds. In the front is Yusif, now clean-shaven as every groom must be when processing toward his bride. Kamal, for his part, dreams simultaneously of music and of the building site. At every checkpoint, al-Jaabari mumbles, "Lo, we fixed before them a barrier and behind them a barrier," and Kawthar smiles, watching the pavement racing by below. We did it! We're on our way there, for real this time. Oh, but will the journey ever end?

••••••

When the ambassador asked why they didn't take the Karm Abu Salem crossing, Yahya had exploded. "You expect us to get an Israeli stamp? Look, Mr. Ambassador, all we're asking for is a simple but official letter to facilitate our passage. It's just a formality. It's not as if it is binding on the embassy or the Egyptian authorities in any way. It's a stupid piece of paper that might help us get around some of the piles of metal strewn along the way."

"Listen, son, whether you end up in heaven or hell, the road passes by death. Regardless of whether Gaza is your paradise or your inferno, the road there doesn't pass by me. Go die somewhere else."

••••••

Hisham Pasha. Ibrahim Beyk. So many soldiers, their faces fixed in jaundiced smiles. *We can't let you in for your own safety. You're in our custody, and this is a war zone.* Standing in the open air, their faces were whipped by cold gusts of wind. Neither pleading nor the unsweetened coffee worked any magic at the Kharrouba checkpoint. They had slipped through all the others as if by magic, but not this one.

Had they hidden the camera properly and had the blond guy not sat by the passenger window and had (fill in the blanks).

Something about them screamed that they were a mass of anger wrapped in love. It was inevitable they would be stopped. And they were.

Back they went.

••••••

"We care for your safety more than for our own citizens'. This is a war zone. Many of our men have been killed here. That's why we can't let you through." So said a plainclothes lieutenant, the highest security official at Kharrouba, the only checkpoint to have stopped us in the long succession beginning with the one right outside Cairo and ending at Checkpoint Impossible: Rafah.

"We're not sure how you managed to get through the earlier checkpoints. You must be ghosts or something. Unfortunately, luck has brought you this far where even ghosts can't get through."

Luck had nothing to do with it, not even remotely: The road to Rafah is a straight shot—a long series of checkpoints with tarmac in between. And Kharrouba was the endpoint of the four-and-a-half hour journey that began in a sand-swept place under a Cairo bridge. The sand would be our faithful companion the entire way.

The Marj terminal swarmed with public transport buses and vehicles. Sa'eed, the driver of the eight-passenger green Mercedes, had asked for 400 Egyptian pounds. As one of us thought this was a steal, we agreed to the price, and when we got to our destination, we gave him 450 pounds, including the obligatory tip—the man had endured our two-hour-long argument with security officials, as well as the cold desert night and the lieutenant's petty humiliations. Along the way, two of us (not knowing the other had done the same) offered him another ten pounds to compensate him for the sum that was the object of a veritable storm of phone calls between Abu Shayma', the garage conductor, and Sa'eed. The other drivers had jumped into the fray and cautioned Sa'eed not to act recklessly when his voice trembled in protest against the controller's levy on each vehicle. "I swear to God, Audeh, he's only supposed to stamp my vehicle's card, but what can I do? I'm the one that does all the work, and he gets a share of the cake!"

Audeh was what Sa'eed called whoever was being friendly toward him, even if the lucky candidate got screwed in the process: In our case, not only was the regular fare for that trip 230 pounds, but in his eagerness to part us with our money, the next day Sa'eed got an extra 100 pounds, just to take us from El-Arish to Rafah. "A special price, I swear, just for you, ya Audeh, because I really like you," he explained—the regular fare for that trip being 40 pounds.

"No sweat, think of it as wealth redistribution," I said as we stopped halfway between El-Arish and Rafah where there was another attempt to send us packing.

"You don't have the required permit from your embassy. I'm sorry, there's nothing I can do for you. We'll notify the local command post and wait for instructions." So we waited, steeped in cigarette smoke, unsweetened coffee, and small talk. To the security men, we were like foundlings, a bunch of writers and artists eager to discuss any topic under the sun in the tedium of their no-man's-land. The encounter was warm in spite of the no-go order.

"Too bad, you were turned down. Try again tomorrow."

Even though tomorrow is an eternity to those who wait, we went back to El-Arish, hopeful.

• • • • • •

There's a white surveillance balloon and three jets scarifying the face of the sky. Soundlessly, a plume of black smoke rises to the right and then another in the middle: ahead, just smoke, and then there she is. A mere arm's length away—no further than a heartbeat or the enveloping smell—lying before your very eyes, the beloved, her hair unfurled along the edge of the shore, white foam lapping against her bare thighs.

Stretch out your hand and you can almost touch her, but before you can feel the shiver of the thrill, walls and barriers go up, and you go down to the ground in the swarm of soldiers. No Entry, No Photography, No Sitting, No Standing, No Loitering,

No Return—and you, a mere cockroach squirming under the avalanche of shoes to your head.

They scattered, trying to conceal themselves amongst the fair-skinned people, some Frenchmen, so as to slip through the metal bars like the desert dust. But even the all-white French breeze couldn't get by the watchful concrete towers of the so-called Rafah Land Port.

••••••

The border. The line that separates here and (t)here. The line between who we were and who we are: passage, wilderness, dispossession.

Slithering like a snake across the tarmac, the sand seeps under our feet and through the barriers where we stand looking for a chink in the phalanx of security men. And Palestine, right there, only meters away. Sand on sand, the sand where they dwell, the very same on which you step. And yet, here it's Egypt and there it's Palestine. Here, we stand pacing, and there, it might as well be another galaxy, forbidden like the fruit of the tree of knowledge. And you, tinier than a grain of sand blown by the wind between the metal barriers.

It's for your own safety. You don't have a permit from your embassy. You're Jordanians, what've you got to do with Gaza? That afternoon, Israeli jets weren't the only ones striking. And they weren't there to surrender to any bombardment. They were there, with all their gear, their ‘oud, their voices, and people all around. Like the fingers of a hand curling into a fist, they gathered around, and broke into song.

We will not lie down and die. Nor will we allow those on the inside to die. Even in death, theirs is an act of not dying. These barriers/crossing-points will not break our bonds: Over there, they remain, be it hollering at the top of their lungs from one flank of the Golan to the other, making their way across the river Jordan, or cleaving the waves on ancient vessels. And we, over here, stand at the crossing with all our sadness.

We shall cross.

2–Mohammad Hamad al-Hunayti

The funeral was a solemn affair. A procession of mourners, Arab delegations, tribal chiefs, and the king himself followed behind the casket mounted on a gun carriage and led by phalanxes of rebels—titans draped in cartridge belts, their shoulder-mounted rifles swinging to the rhythm of their vigorous steps.

Under the blanket of the sky, their ‘abayas spread out on the ground in front of Mohammad al-Hunayti’s house on the flank of Jabal al-Lweibdeh, hundreds of mourners awaited the arrival of the casket from Haifa. Salvos of gunfire erupted as soon as it came into view, making its way down the road from Salt. The martyr had returned: it was a day worthy of the Last Judgment.

Abdelhalim al-Nimer and the men of Salt had insisted that the martyr remain in their midst two more days. "The man is our son," they had cried. How dear they held him, cherished as the apple of an eye, and they accompanied him all the way to Amman.

• • • • • •

Every night, the German shepherd stands on the perimeter wall of the house in Abu 'Alanda looking out to the West. The dog, which Mohammad al-Hamad had brought back from Haifa on his last trip, begins to howl, crying bitter, heart-wrenching tears.

"Kill the dog. Mohammad will never return." So said the mukhtar of the al-Hunayti clan, Abu Khaled, through clenched teeth.

• • • • • •

The shortest route follows a straight line, and that is how they proceeded along the coastal road. Bound for Haifa, they had set off from Beirut in a procession of vehicles laden with weapons, including two trucks piled with explosives.

The British officer at Ras al-Naqura sent word of their arrival, and when they got to Acre, the inhabitants warned him:

"Mohammad Beyk, the Zionists may have gotten wind of your convoy. There is news that they tried to ambush you in Ain Sara near Nahariyya and failed. The coastal road will be your undoing. Forget this route and go back to Beirut. From there, you can go to Damascus and then onto Irbid and Haifa. It'll take three days, but it will save your life." Others suggested that he ship the weapons by sea, or at the very least, stay with them overnight in Acre.

"The safest route may take three days, and the churning of the sea is never without a wave," Mohammad Beyk replied. "But I left Haifa alone on her balcony waiting for the seafarer who only days ago crossed rivers of tarmac toward the North. The seafarer's beloved never sleeps, and she doesn't like waiting," he added. "Ya ikhwan, Haifa is without arms. Those marauders will not wait. If they lay their hands on Haifa, it will kill me just the same. Let me die on her bosom trying to defend her rather than watch her being overrun from afar." He left for the South and never looked back.

••••••

He was shrewd, smart, and educated, and the slightly disfigured Englishman had been doing the rounds of the tribes to enlist their sons into his army.

Mohammad al-Hunayti was the son of the region's ruling pasha under the Ottomans—a man who'd been the terror of the bandits and thieves that were the Turkish army's foot soldiers. His mother was a Kurdish Damascene who insisted he get an education, and sent him to study under a Circassian tutor at the entrance to the Great Mosque in Amman. Muhammad was never to be found sleeping without a book across his face. His eyes sparkled with intelligence as he debated and argued, and Glubb Pasha recruited him forthwith. He was quick to prove his military acumen and was appointed an officer in Haifa.

As it behooved any intelligent young man whose brain the British and the Zionists drilled into day in and day out, the officer siphoned the weapons that fell into his hands to the city's inhabitants. Later, he assembled his men and addressed them as follows: "At night, slip off your military uniforms, dress in civvies, and go train the people of Haifa in warfare." And so it was.

Since it behooves a military field commander to know his enemy and understand what is required of him to mete out defeat, he wove bonds of blood with his comrades in arms among the rebels. The handsome Bedouin met with all the local leaders—Rashid al-Hajj Ibrahim, Suroor Barham, al-Abed al-Khatib, Abu Nimer, Mohammad Abu Aziz, Abu Ali Dalloul, Hassan Shiblaq, Abu Ibrahim Odeh, Rashed al-Zafari, Nimer al-Mansour, Jameel Bakeer, and Yousef al-Hayek—and he became one of them.

Did I say *became*? That is false, because he had been one of them ever since screaming his way into the world at the desert's edge. And they were of him from the time he had drawn his first breath.

"You are Jordanian, Mohammad Beyk, what have you got to do with the Palestinians?" Glubb had asked, waving his spies' reports in the air.

"Ya basha," Mohammad had replied, "you are the ones who drew the boundaries of this land. Before you, there was neither Palestine nor Jordan, neither Syria nor Lebanon. Until you came along, we traded in the souks of Damascus and wintered on the shores of the Mediterranean. Defending Haifa is defending my village, Abu 'Alanda, ya basha. Here, take these insignia of yours. I have no use for them anymore. The freedom fighter's badge is far superior."

Rifle slung on his shoulder, and cartridge belts draped across his chest, he came back from that confrontation and took off his military uniform. He donned the rebels' garb and became the high commander of harakat al-jihad al-muqaddas (the Sacred Jihad Movement) for the Haifa district. After that day, no one would ever trample him underfoot nor would he ever lower his head again, were it to receive the crown of a monarch.

How many a king, unjust, tyrannical, and headstrong
His garments forever dragging on the ground
His bones no more than the dust of rusted metal
Trampled underfoot by all.

After that day, no one ever trampled him underfoot: He unified the city's defenders under his command and deployed the small army of 350 combatants across ten different sectors, each with a commander of its own. Its head resting in the lap of the Mediterranean and within reach of the Gulf's embrace, mild and gentle Haifa turned into a saber-toothed, bare-clawed tigress, and the men who had issued from her womb would not disavow her, whose bosom had nursed them.

• • • • • •

Motorcycles shot by like lightning bolts, followed soon after by barrels rolling down the road toward them in a hail of gunfire and hand grenades. Mohammad al-Hunayti instructed his chauffeur to proceed, and the driver of the first truck followed suit, but the barrage of fire was so intense that there was a skirmish.

The last truck in the convoy turned around and headed back to Acre. The rebels ran toward their leader who was lying on the ground cradling his rifle. Dodging bullets and rolling in the little craters formed by their impact, Suroor Barham crawled on his belly to reach him. "Mohammad Beyk," he said, shaking him roughly, "answer me, brother." But Mohammad spoke not a word and, as never before, remained completely still. A trickle of blood no thicker than a thread issued from between his lips. Mohammad al-Hunayti had returned to Haifa.

From the corner of his eye, Suroor could see the Palmach fighters clambering up the truck and neutralizing it. He felt around his pocket and located it. "Beloved, today is the day of our betrothal," he said, pulling out the pin and running. Red gouges appeared on his back, and little dart-like pins ripped his entrails, but a light hand carried him, as if the two feet propelling him were not his own. He reached the truck and exploded.

The inhabitants of northern Palestine and southern Lebanon as far north as Sidon swore that on the evening of Wednesday March 17, 1948, the earth had trembled below their feet, that their houses had shaken, and that a man had been seen flying through the air and landing on top of one of the railcars going toward Acre.

• • • • • •

"Hey, Abdel-Razzak...Abdel-Razzak," screamed a child outside the door, "your father's picture is in all the papers. He fell in battle." The headline, "Martyr who Stunned the Zionists," in red lettering, took up the entire front page of *al-Difaa'*. "On their airwaves," the report said, "they described him as a menace unlike any other Arab commander." In a traditional gesture of grief, his mother, Umm Mohammad, upended the coffeepots on the ground, and ululations filled the air.

When they uncovered the body before his relatives, his face looked just as it did in the photograph hanging on the wall. If anything, it was more radiant. There were some who said they could smell the aroma of oranges exuding from his body.

Nothing in him was altered other than a line of bullet holes on his chest. “A true hero, my child, you never gave them your back.” His mother kissed his forehead, and the funeral procession set out.

Right behind the casket marched rows of titans draped in cartridge belts, shoulder-mounted rifles moving to the rhythm of their vigorous steps, a child weaving between their legs and tripping over their feet. One of them pushed him roughly. “Go play elsewhere,” he yelled.

“Don’t push me away, that’s my dad,” protested the child. The man pounded his head with his fists and wept, and then he hoisted the boy up onto his shoulders.

• • • • • •

[Communiqué from Haifa City National Committee]

March 19, 1948

Death Notice

Herewith, a convoy of heroes that met their maker in service to the nation. Haifa City National Committee is grieved to announce to our honorable Arab umma the death of its brightest and dearest sons and bravest soldiers, as follows:

1. Mohammad Beyk Hamad al-Hunayti, the fearless commander of the Haifa garrison;
2. Suroor Barham (Abu Mahmoud), deputy commander;
3. Fakhreddine Abdel-Wahed (Egypt);
4. Omar Khaled al-Khateeb;
5. Ahmad Khader Musa;
6. Ahmad Wajeeh Rahhal;
7. Yusif al-Taweel;
8. Ali Kabbar;
9. Hassan Salameh (Jordan);
10. 'Atallah Salameh (Jordan);
11. Ali Shujaa';
12. Mohammad Mustafa Khalil;
13. Albert the Armenian.

They fell on the battlefield following an ambush at around three o'clock on the afternoon of March 17, 1948.
We mourn these heroes of the Arab nation in the knowledge that the blood they have shed will never be forgotten.

••••••

[Chronology]

March 17, 1948: death in battle of the leader of the armed resistance in Haifa, Mohammad Hamad al-Hunayti, and his deputy, Suroor Barham, following an ambush by the Zionist Palmach forces on a convoy of weapons under their command.

April 6-8, 1948: failure of the attack on Kibbutz Mishmar HaEmek, on the Haifa-Jenin road, by the forces of Jaysh al-Inqadh (the pan-Arab volunteer force) under the command of Fawzi al-Qawuqji. Zionist forces carry out a counterattack in which they are able to cut off scores of Arab villages as well as the outlying areas of Haifa.

April 8, 1948: Death of commander Abd al-Qader al-Husseini in the battle of al-Qastal, and fall of the village.

April 9, 1948: Massacre of Deir Yassin.

April 22, 1948: Fall of Haifa to the Haganah.

May 14, 1948: David Ben-Gurion proclaims the establishment of the State of Israel.

3–Second Attempt

Between the grim concrete wall and the fields of red poppies, where a thin line separates life and death, old, cracked fingers dug through the soil, clinging to the edges of the ground like claws. From under them rose a body, tall and lofty as a mountain, its two arms straight as rifles poised to fire, legs like columns carved from the rocks of the lilac hills, a face like a city by the shore keeping vigil for her seafaring lover.

Mohammad Hamad al-Hunayti dusted himself off. Looking around, he found numerous people staring at him, mouths agape.

"Who are you?" his warm voice exclaimed.

"We are the blood that has stopped flowing after misery-induced strokes blocked our arteries," said the injured man.

"We are the tree branches that have extended to the neighbor's house, which the neighbor cut and stacked to dry behind the wall," said the mother.

"We are the ones who may not be visited or embraced because they say that we are not who we are," said the organizer of the delegation trying to cross.

Is that what we have come to? I've been gone only 62 years and this is what it has come to, Mohammad Hamad al-Hunayti thought to himself, but when he screamed, all that came out was a roar. As the many fingers emerged from the soil, towering bodies split the earth, dusted themselves off, looked around, and embraced each other like long-lost friends: Izzedine al-Qassam, Ziad Tanash, Rachel Corrie, Abd al-Qader al-Husseini, Wafa' Idriss, Firas al-Ajlouni, Faris Odeh, Kayed al-Mufleh al-Obeidat, Dalal al-Mughrabi, Ahmad Abdelaziz, Suroor Barham, Sa'eed al-'Aass, Ahmad al-Majali. "How's it going? Long time." "Yeah, really too long."

As they set off, the earth shakes and with every tremor, hundreds, no, thousands, and then millions emerge, and every language under the sun from every corner of the world also sets forth; with every step, the walls and the roadblocks fall away, and they cross. With every step, the villages and houses are returned, the names and the memories recovered, the weddings and dab-kehs come back, and the smell of oranges fills the air.

They all met on the shore of Haifa, all those who had crossed border posts and boundaries, roadblocks and walls, and all those who had come from the sea, sailing on ancient boats. They danced and danced until it was light, until the grass was brought forth and the herb had yielded seed and the fruit trees bore fruit all across the face of the earth, which had been void and formless and covered in darkness. A new day had sprung.

[The Book of Zechariah, Chapter 15]

I have come from east of the river. I sound my roar, the roar of a lion, and then cross. Not by the might of the sword, but with my own two feet. And lo my friends appear; from the soil below they come forth, from the houses they come forth, from every nation of the earth they come forth to walk by my side. The earth shakes under their footsteps, and the walls crack open. Death shall be the lot of those that have slain lives by the sword. And fire shall burn those who unleashed rivers of blood. And the Lord of hosts shall call to his people: I come with fire, with my chariots like a whirlwind, to render my anger with fury and my rebuke with flames of fire. But the earth shakes, and the Lord's people scatter and run. And the Lord of hosts calls to his people: I have given you a land on which you did not toil and cities you built not, and you dwell in them; of the vineyards and olive groves which you planted not, yet do you eat. Your male and female slaves are to come from the nations around you; from them you may buy slaves. You may also buy of the children of the strangers that live among you and of those of their lineage that are born in your land, who are with you, and they shall be your possession. You may bequeath them to your children after you to inherit as a possession forever. But the earth shakes and the Lord's people scatter and run. On this day, people shall cross from the four corners of the earth, and that day shall be as the day of the locust, as the tower of Babel. Every tongue shall appear, the kingdom of justice shall be formed, and the kingdom of the sword that benighted every nation shall lie in ruins and perish.

[MUSEUM OF FOUND OBJECTS: DISCARDED PHOTO ALBUM 2]

Mohammad Hamad al-Hunayti in military uniform, 1946

Mahmoud Abu Salem (the flying man) with al-Hunayti's grandchildren, 1986

NOTES:

News brief: "A delegation of Jordanian writers and artists was prevented from entering Gaza through the Egyptian Rafah crossing on 2/17/2009. The delegation, calling itself Jordanian Intellectuals for Gaza, was part of an international movement to break the siege on the densely-populated strip following Operation Cast Lead, Israel's massive assault on Gaza. The group, made up of Hisham Bustani (writer), Mohammad Nasrallah (painter), Kamal Khalil (musician), Ayed Nab'a (film director), Abdel-Rahman al-Jaabari (caricaturist), Kawthar 'Arar (journalist), Yusef Abu-Jaysh (writer), and Yahya Abu Safi (researcher) remained stranded at the Rafah border crossing for three days; there, they staged a protest in solidarity with the people of Gaza, erecting a display of caricatures in front of the crossing. They are expected back in Amman, tomorrow." *al-Ghad*, Feb. 20, 2009.

"We fixed before them a barrier ..." is Verse 9 of Sura 36, Ya Sin. (The Qur'an: A New Translation by Tarif Khalidi, New York: Viking Press, 2008.)

How many a king...: those lines of Nabati verse were composed by Muhammad Hamad al-Hunayti himself.

The flying man was Mahmoud Abu Salem the personal bodyguard of Mohammad al-Hunayti and the sole survivor from the ambush operation. Propelled by the force of the explosion, he landed on the roof of a railcar on its way to Acre.

Izzedine al-Qassam was born in 1882 in Jableh, in what is now Syria. Condemned to death by the French Mandate authorities for his anti-colonial resistance activities, he left Jableh, and made his way to Haifa where he organized armed resistance to the British Mandate authorities and Zionist colonizers in Palestine.

Ziad Tanash, from Howwara, Jordan. He joined the Lebanon-based Quwwat al-Ansar, and was killed in 1976 in an Israeli air strike. The Palestinian poet

Izzidin al- Manasra mourned him with the poem *We shrouded him in green*, later famously set to music by Marcel Khalife.

Rachel Corrie was a U.S. member of an international solidarity group with Palestine. She was born in 1979 in Olympia, Washington, and was killed by an Israeli D9 Caterpillar bulldozer as she tried to prevent it from demolishing a Palestinian home in Gaza on March 16, 2003.

Abd al-Qader al-Husseini (b. 1910) was the leader of the armed resistance in the Jerusalem district during the 1948 war. He was killed in the battle of al-Qastal, on April 8, 1948.

Wafa' Idriss was the first female suicide bomber of the al-Aqsa Intifada (2nd Intifada) that began in 2000. One day after Israeli F-16s had strafed the Palestinian cities of Gaza, Tulkarm, and Nablus, she blew herself up in occupied West Jerusalem on January 27, 2002.

Firas al-Ajlouni (b. in Anjara, in Jordan's northern district of Ajloun) was a Jordanian air force pilot, who single-handedly faced off an Israeli air force squadron during the 1967 war. He was killed by Israeli fire the last time he launched into flight on June 5, 1967.

Faris Odeh was the 14-year-old boy killed by Israeli gunfire at the Karni crossing in Gaza on November 8, 2000. A photo of him hurling a stone at an Israeli tank ten days earlier became an iconic representation of Palestinian resistance to the Israeli occupation.

Kayed al-Mufleh al-Obeidat, aka the Falcon of Palestine, was born in Kufr Soom near Irbid, in what is modern-day northern Jordan. He was killed in 1920 while leading an attack on British forces in the region of Samakh in what is now occupied Palestine.

Dalal al-Moghrabi (b. 1958 in the Sabra refugee camp, Lebanon) headed Operation Kamal Adwan. With her squad of fedayeen, she hijacked a bus on the coastal road between Haifa and Tel Aviv, hoisting the Palestinian flag along the highway. A special unit of the Israeli army, led by Ehud Barak (later prime minister), put an end to the operation.

Ahmad Abdelaziz is Egypt's national hero from the 1948 war. He resigned his own military commission to lead the volunteer Egyptian battalion in Palestine. He is buried north of Bethlehem.

Suroor Barham (b. 1930) was a follower of Izzedine al-Qassam. He joined the Haifa garrison as Mohammad al-Hunayti's deputy commander, and was killed on March 17, 1948 in the Palmach ambush of al-Hunayti's arms convoy.

Sa'eed al-'Aass (b. in Hama, present-day Syria) was a leader of the 1925 Syrian Revolt against the French colonial authorities. He was also active in the anti-British revolt in Palestine and was killed on October 6, 1936, in the hills between Jerusalem and Hebron.

Ahmad al-Majali was born in 1963 in al-Karak, Jordan, and died in 1983, fighting on the front between Israel and Lebanon following the 1982 Israeli invasion of the country. The poet Ibrahim Nasrallah wrote "Love Song to the Martyr of al-Karak" in his memory.

Chapter 15 of the Book of Zechariah is a fragment of text found in the Qumran Caves along with other texts of the Essene, known as the Qumran Caves Scrolls. It was not canonized in the Hebrew Bible, the Tanakh.

LIKE A DREAM

ABOVE THE CLOUDS, BEHIND THE GLASS, OUTSIDE THE BODY

Between al-Shawbak's enchanting springtime and the beautiful girls of Amman, he discovered the world. He was branded the perennial lover, the eternal romantic.

Always on the precipice of infatuation, he views Woman as a mythical creature, a sweeping metaphysical force beyond life itself, beyond Time or History—a magnificent torrent to be swept up in, a torrent his whole being can drown in, submerged from head to toe, with complete abandon.

He simply wants to be engulfed in her waters—just like that, without the slightest reciprocation or exchange—and to yield to the torrent's overpowering force as it rushes over him.

• • • • • •

"Is that what love is?" I asked him, wondering why he was hovering so stubbornly close to the window.

"Through the doors, pain, sadness, and loneliness rush in/ And through the windows, we watch the moving clouds, the passing beauties, the fluttering gesture of hope." That's what he was thinking, but he said, "*Love is being buried underground, hearing from below the voice of the one you dream of, and emerging to return to life's embrace.*" Instantly, he turned into a beam of light that began refracting between the window and a mirror hanging on the wall.

I lit a cigarette, blowing the smoke into the air, and he appeared clearly. "Love is not some absolute," I told him. "It's not a metaphysical substance that we imbibe or that is descended upon us like divine rain; it's not some kind of redemptive nirvana that we attain through a mystical process of transcendence. Love takes place in historical time, not outside of it; it happens between people, between two individuals. It's not some abstract relationship between Presence and Absence."

"*Love is my most beautiful details, my noblest battles, the boundless source of energy,*" replied the light-beam, to which I answered: "Love is a dynamic, it ebbs and it flows, it peaks and subsides, it acts and is acted upon. It is not a constant from eternity to eternity." He stopped at the window suddenly, his front bumping into his back, and fell to the ground like a wounded falcon.

I jumped up and ran toward him. I struggled to say something but the words wouldn't come out, and when I reached my hand cautiously to where the falcon was bleeding, it rose up and flew off, landing on the window, wounds healed and beak to the sky. Addressing an imaginary audience, he said: "*Love, ladies and gentlemen, is my High Dam, its waves rushing over my heart so that life may go forth. In love, you are clean of heart, pure of tongue, spirit absolute, not body carnal. In love, you are transformed into colossal spirit.*"

From behind the glass, young women dressed in bright colors teetered on the sidewalk, looking up coyly. Some winked, others flashed smiles that quickened the blood with the thrill of desire. A carnival of sex stuffed into tight-fitting jeans, beamed across Bluetooth wavelengths and Facebook pages. Despite the hammering of the falcon's beak and the fluttering of his wings, the transparent glass barrier was unyielding. It would not dissolve. "The eye is without memory/ Only the hand remembers." The falcon remained memory-less. "*The body is mere carnality, but the immensity of spirit is yours if you love,*" he said.

When I invited him to leave, he said nothing. I begged him to shed his feathers and his beak, and to come back with a mouth and a tongue and bare arms, but my words fell to the ground before reaching him. "As the storm blows about him/ He joins his palms and says/ All those feathers, but not enough to form a wing."

• • • • • •

I looked up toward the window, and there he was, lean and naked, twisting and turning, pressing his body against the glass; I, for my part, dissolved into the torrents of young women dressed in bright colors.

NOTES:

"The eye is without memory/ Only the hand remembers," is a line from Nusayyef al-Nasiri's poetry collection, *Ard khadra' mithl abwab al-sanah.*

"Through the doors, pain..." and **"As the storm blows..."** are lines of poetry by Basim al-Mir'abi, an Iraqi poet living in Sweden.

This story is built around an incomplete discussion with Mansour al-Tourah about an essay he wrote entitled "Talking About Love." The **statements in italics** are excerpted from the essay.

[MUSEUM OF FOUND OBJECTS: A DISCARDED LETTER]

Dear Mansour,

Being in love is a state of completion between the lover and the beloved, one in which they complement one another. There is no place here for sacrifice or compromise: how can we love another whose being has been truncated?

Love is a state of mutual awareness, a heightened state I might say, where the senses reach the pinnacle of their expression and the body tenses in response. Thus, love is a physical state: it is eyes that sparkle, mouths that banter, the shiver of touch, the meeting of minds. There is no love outside the body, and there is no body outside History; the body is in the world and not above it, outside it, or somehow transcendent. Even the celibate Platonic lover must have a beloved who is embodied, who is made of flesh and blood. There is no such thing as an absolute Platonic state where woman does not exist, or love does not occur.

By body, I don't mean the body of a woman. I mean the body as causality, as locus, vessel, existence itself—be it an idea in the mind, earthly oppression, terrestrial geography, or an as-yet not fully realized history.

"And truly what is a person besides mind?" al-Farabi tells us. The mind is the highest expression of the body, it is the epicenter of the body, and the senses are its instruments. What is this "spirit," you speak of, absent the "body" or "mind." To your way of looking at it, the body remains a lowly thing—mere "carnality," an object of contempt—while the mind is veiled.

Spirits are in love, you say? What are these loving spirits that have no eyes to see the beloved, or ears to hear his words, no nostrils with which to smell, or hands with which to caress, or a mind with which to understand him? A spirit without body is the very definition of nihilism. If you despise the body, you cannot dance or write or listen to music. All these things derive from the body and are perceived by it.

••••••

Mansour,

When you leapt fully conscious (and maybe with your subconscious too) into the torrent of metaphysical love, erupting into it with all your being and your senses, did you think that you were perhaps undergoing some mystical experience? The mystic's highest goal is to cast aside the veil of ignorance and to remain present, feeling oneness with the divine Self. That is why the mystic looks to the divine light, bathes in it, and identifies with it, relinquishing (or maybe, more aptly, sacrificing) his sense of self in order to achieve Unity.

But you, my friend, who are impelled to dissolve in Woman's sweeping torrent, have forgotten that obliteration and mystical dissolution in the divine Self are by necessity functions of a relationship between nonequals: the lower, limited self (of the mystic) dissolves in the eternal, unlimited Self (of the divine). For the mystic, it's a matter of "transcendence," a plus, if you will, wherein the veil is lifted and perfect knowledge is attained. But man and woman are "equal" on the ladder of hierarchies, neither of them more elevated than the other or more exalted whether through dissolution in the other, or through self-obliteration; and neither of them is a rushing torrent for the other to be swept up by, and to which they surrender their very being or relinquish their own will.

Submission in a relationship is the mirror image of sadomasochistic duality. Masochism is the "dissolution" of the self in the beloved (whether man or woman); it involves self-annihilation and the surrender of one's will to another who is equal in their humanity and existence. It's neither for a woman to be swept up in the rushing torrent of a man, nor for a man to be swept up in the rushing torrent of a woman.

Love is not masochism. Your view of Woman as the object of your surrender and submission is masochistic. Did you not say with your own tongue: "Love is the feeling that causes one's heart to beat and to suffer, although the suffering is pleasurable." Pleasurable pain? Taking pleasure in suffering is nothing if not the definition of masochism.

Do you remember Khaled, the narrator of Dhakirat al-jassad? As he dissolves into the illusory beloved, his name practically disappears from the story altogether; he considers her the center of his life after only a few brief encounters, he feels she has become his reason for living, which is what leads to his disastrous fate. "How could your sadistic bent not have aroused my suspicions that day, and how did I not anticipate the later crimes you would commit as you honed your other weapons?" he tells her. "I hadn't expected that you would aim them at me one day. That's why I smiled at your words, and that's when I became smitten with you. In such circumstances, we (men) cannot resist the madness of enchantment, be it with our own killer!"

Khaled, the masochistic lover, doesn't resist. He keeps moving toward his killer. Even after he acknowledges that it is masochism, he savors the suffering she visits upon him. To the point of addiction. If you questioned him, he would say: But it is pleasurable suffering.

That is love?

••••••

My dear friend,

Your view of love obliterates the self, the will, and the mind in the name of metaphysical delusions: you have made of love a "self" of its own, and of women some kind of absolute. That's a kind of reverse chauvinism: the flip side of the prevailing view that men's worth lies merely in their being men—and not because they are good, or bad, human beings—while women's worth is not inherent to their womanhood, period, but somehow attributable to the merit of their acts.

Are Mourid Barghouti's two women equal in your view? "The woman who knows all the silverware shops in Paris/ and complains/ The woman who weeps every Thursday in five cemeteries/ and stands unbowed."

There is no equivalence between the two. Meaning that there is no absolute value that is unbound by historicity—or to echo Ibrahim al-Koni's enigmatic observation that "the condition for freedom is to forsake women," and men for that matter, insofar as they too are considered absolutes and not objectively intelligible. The only way to free ourselves from this sexist chauvinism, this metaphysical defeatism, is for us to interact with each other in all our fullness as human beings.

Furthermore, my friend, you contradict yourself: when you define Woman simply as mother/sister/lover, the remnants of patriarchy are clearly exposed. When your Woman is merely the mother of a man, his sister, or his beloved, notwithstanding your lofty and eloquent words, there is no place for her outside the ambit of a man or his attachment to her. The Woman/Goddess whom you worship has just fallen.

••••••

Dear Mansour,

The road to love is long and difficult, it is analogous to the path to Knowledge and to the way of mystical transcendence: it involves searching, seeking, and discovering; it goes beyond the reflection of young women passing by behind the window-glass. Nor is it a matter of heartbeats being kindled one day and subsiding the next, like some desert flower that erupts into bloom after a sudden rain.

The falcon soaring above the clouds, and over the treetops and mountain peaks, does not touch the deluge of fire rippling below.

With my affection and esteem,

Hisham

NOTE:

The two women are from Mourid Barghouti's collection of poems, *Taala al-shataat.*

NICOTINE

Sitting enveloped in a cloud of smoke was not one of his favorite pleasures, but today was hers. Usually, he was the one to decide where they would meet, but this time he'd left it up to her.

She sat across from him, her face stiff as an untouched canvas stretched on its frame. She cut her food methodically with her fork and knife, placed it in her mouth, chewed, and swallowed without the minutest change in her non-expression.

"Your dispassion is boundless," he told her. "Like the polar ice plains. Do you feel no pleasure as the food oozes onto your tongue and palate? Don't you smell it or delight in its colors? Although not everyone realizes it, eating is such a sensual experience. Like music, but more so because taste is a really neglected sense."

"I lost all sensation a while ago, one year ago to be precise," she said, tossing her hair back.

"Then you're no longer human. If music doesn't affect you, and neither does appetizing food that is artfully prepared, and you don't react to a painting, or your skin doesn't tingle when a tongue slides along your neck...what is left?"

"The hookah."

••••••

The man had opened the world to her and she had become infatuated with him. He'd lavished on her passion, vigor, and jealousy to the point of exhaustion, and after wringing every last drop of juice out of her, so that she was stripped of her senses, he discarded her. She had become a body that was sealed, but only on the inside: a white circular chamber floating in space.

••••••

"There's nothing left in me," she said a few seconds later, as if reappearing after being in another world. He'd had to snap his fingers for her to come back to him. "Six whole years. I hadn't ever been with anyone before him, I'd never done the wild teenage thing, or lavished my emotions on anyone until I met him; I was virginal in every sense when he found me."

A gaggle of young women in the background then stood up laughing and broke into a loud rendition of "Happy Birthday."

She didn't even turn around, and continued looking straight ahead at the colored wall in front of her as the eye stinging smoke streamed from her exhalations, thickening the air.

"You are victimizing yourself, climbing the ladder of your illusions and then falling down and feeling hurt. He's not the problem. He was clear with you and went on his way. But you remain as tightly wound as the bud you first gifted him, going around and around like in an endless maze. Hiba, there's nothing on the wall in front of you but circles, without beginning or end. Don't even try to find your way out, they're like whorls of dry quicksand just sucking you in."

She didn't respond. She was feeling dizzy, and closed her eyes for an instant; it felt as if everything was spinning around, and she was being pulled downward. It was a nice sensation, a feeling of total surrender, of emptiness, of having no willpower, like a universe devoid of gravitational pull. A parallel universe where the laws of physics didn't apply, where there was only one principle: endless space and nothingness.

She opened her eyes suddenly, startled by the banging of the coffee cup against the glass tabletop, and the apologies of the waiter. She was still in the café, and he was still studying her silently, and the birthday girls carrying on in the background were getting louder and louder. She looked crestfallen, and felt her insides were being ripped by vicious worms, and then a wave of nausea rushed over her.

She fought back the heaving of her stomach—she was a well-brought up girl and wasn't about to throw up all over a café floor in front of people. She took a drag from the hookah, everything went numb, and with the next exhalation, she came back around.

"You know, I don't enjoy the taste of anything anymore, except for the hookah. It's the only thing I enjoy. With every inhalation, the smoke seeps into me, my very pores drink it in, and I feel good. It's my only pleasure, my only remaining sense experience."

"Like having sex with a hookah?" he said, smiling.

"Like it's sucking on me."

• • • • • •

The extended arm withdraws little by little, and she sinks into the hot sand. She has no desire to raise her hand and no longer even looks up. She pulls deeply on the hookah and becomes weightless.

[Of a sleeping man's visions]

Everything is surrounded by emptiness. No gravitational pull or mass here. Everything light, endlessly light, unbearably light.

His hand moves to the tumbler, which gradually recedes as a slightly viscous red liquid appears in amoeba-like formations floating in the air. He grabs the tumbler, flings it up (is there such a thing as "up"?), harnessing the amoebic substance into the trajectory of his mouth, and then swallows.

In that instant, his vision is heightened, he sees what is unseen, and sees into what can be seen. His ears catch the soft sounds of a song playing in the background: "I've been living a lie, there's nothing inside." "A lie?" he asks, as he watches her passing before him. His eyes follow her and she turns slowly, her legs shooting up like those of a synchronized swimmer on the surface of the water, and the soft music turns into a monotonous din.

Finally, a sign of life. He sees droplets of sweat sliding on her skin like water slithering on wax. His eyes gleam, and he glides toward her (is there such a thing as "toward her"?). He has to find her, to pull her out, to kiss her, to have sex with her, and ejaculate his viscous fluid deep inside her. A Big Bang would result from their friction, an expansion of mass that takes place in the depth of a void, as semen explodes in the confines of her womb. A universe might arise.

When he gets to her and extends his arms, there is nothing to grab onto but the palms of his own two hands. She continues to twirl slowly, as his momentum takes him right through her, and her right through him, and total silence reigns.

ORCHESTRA

[First movement]

She was seated at the black piano. The music had evaporated from her head, and only crooked melodies stumbled from her fingers. When she turned around, his eyes were looking straight into hers, and the kiss he blew into the air teased her lips.

When she placed her slender fingers inside his mouth, the crookedness of the melodies receded; and when their two bodies joined, the place reverberated with music.

[Second movement]

In the hall, there was complete silence—other than for the speaker's stammering voice; and for the early protestations of a baby, whose victorious utterances propelled his mother outside; and for the ringing of the cellphone in the back, when the audience learned of the beloved's name and that "Encounter between Byzantine and Arab Civilizations: Samples of their Poetry" was simply the cover for the lovers' planned tryst.

It was her turn now. He stopped noticing the heavy breathing of the couple behind him; the brassy woman's explosive clapping at her son's first recitation of poetry in public (never mind that he didn't understand it, what really mattered was the extra grade in class); the feigned interest of the security detachment; and even the glaring look of the Almighty Leader staring menacingly from the frame hanging in the middle of the hall.

It was her turn: the cadence slid into place, and the words flowed in lilac streams across the podium and between the seats. Now alone, he bathed in the fields of his childhood, scaling the clouds of his longing and scattering like flower petals on the warm breeze.

She carried him far away, to the distant place where tears swelled into torrents, and when he left hurriedly to go to his car, her smiling gaze bid him goodbye, blue had cleaved from blue, and color saturated everything: the speaker, the Almighty Leader's portrait, the security men, and all of the phonies in the hall.

With him, in the back seat of the car, was the couple that had sat behind him in the hall, while she slipped into the passenger seat to scatter her colors along the pavement.

[Third movement]

Afterwards, she'd sat in his lap while they read what they could in the way of poetic verses, wrapping their bodies around the music of the words:

The ballerina, who had tumbled from her lips only moments earlier, leapt into the air and snaked across the winding river of fire on the floor. Naked, she circled the perimeter of the body swollen with desire, ascending toward her writer who sat god-like and aloof upon the sofa (or so she thought) where he counted each breath and gathered falling stars, fortunetellers' signs, and what to the listening ear are ciphers of inspiration, packing them all into the jumble of his brain to conjure them up with ink on the desert of parched white paper.

But her writer—the one who is contaminated by minds outside his own, and chafes against bodies made of flesh, igniting the brazier's spark that lights the coal-stack, propelling the driving wheels which overturn the rusty engine of time. That writer of hers was not the One, the Unparalleled, the Everlasting. He was hewing his way through a forest of desire, erupting from pomegranate breasts, gulping down the liquor of saliva, and biting on the stretch of alabaster that led to the promontory of bliss and down to the delta of pleasure. That writer of hers generated fire, piercing the Mother's grass with the Father's flint until their creamy froth mixed.

The ballerina was furious. She raged and she screamed, then realized that her feet rested on the cadence of the two bodies, that her dance was born of their climax, that the melodies she held aloft rose and fell to the rhythm of the gasps cascading from her lips and his.

The ballerina understood that her resurgence dwelled in the fevered delirium of the two joined bodies.

••••••

The night lit up by love was over. The ballerina folded herself back into the white pages and lay down to sleep between the words. She would rise again—the fortune-tellers had told her so—but only when poetry became soft fingertips prying open shirt buttons.

VODKA AT THE SEASIDE

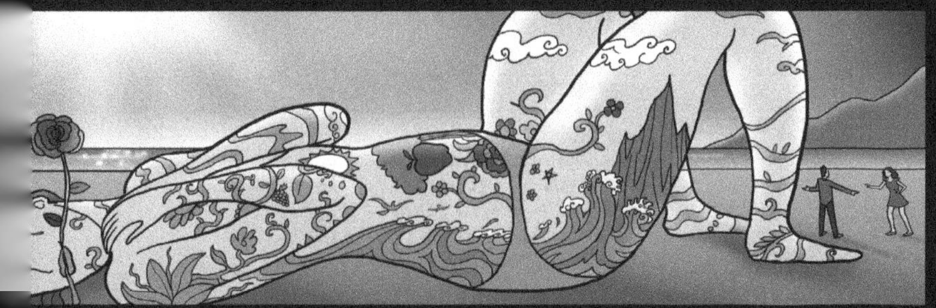

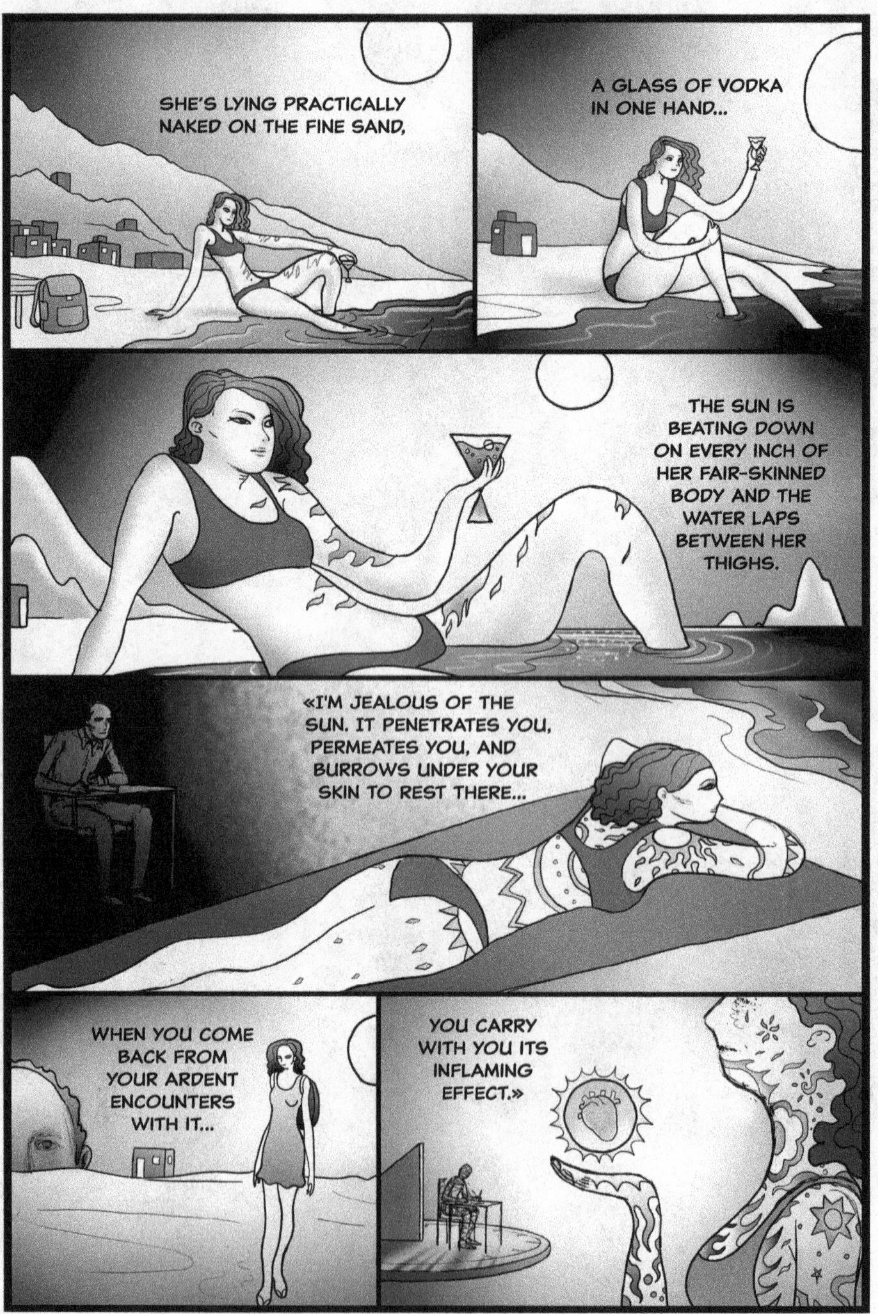
SHE'S LYING PRACTICALLY NAKED ON THE FINE SAND,
A GLASS OF VODKA IN ONE HAND...
THE SUN IS BEATING DOWN ON EVERY INCH OF HER FAIR-SKINNED BODY AND THE WATER LAPS BETWEEN HER THIGHS.
«I'M JEALOUS OF THE SUN. IT PENETRATES YOU, PERMEATES YOU, AND BURROWS UNDER YOUR SKIN TO REST THERE...
WHEN YOU COME BACK FROM YOUR ARDENT ENCOUNTERS WITH IT...
YOU CARRY WITH YOU ITS INFLAMING EFFECT.»

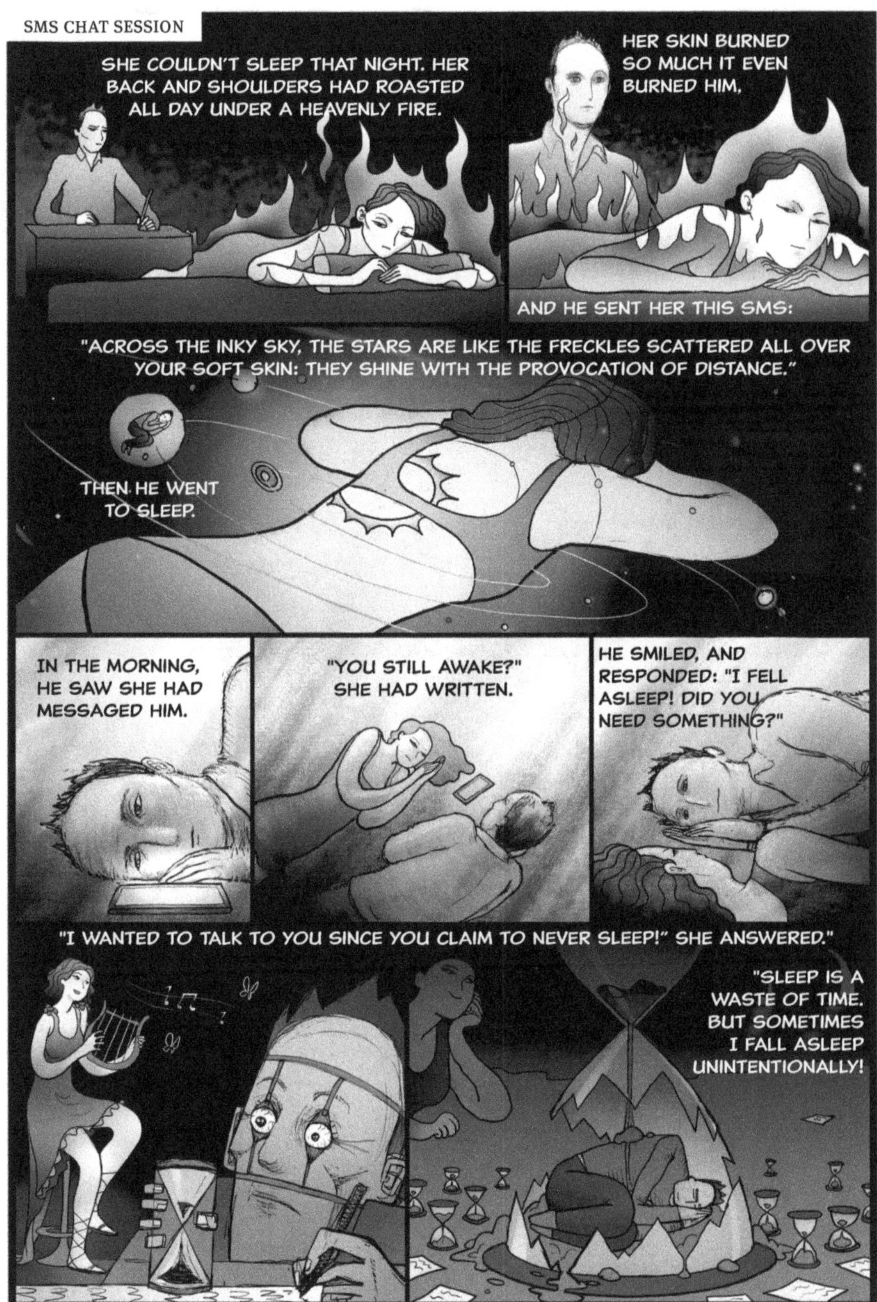
SMS CHAT SESSION
SHE COULDN'T SLEEP THAT NIGHT. HER BACK AND SHOULDERS HAD ROASTED ALL DAY UNDER A HEAVENLY FIRE.
HER SKIN BURNED SO MUCH IT EVEN BURNED HIM,
AND HE SENT HER THIS SMS:
"ACROSS THE INKY SKY, THE STARS ARE LIKE THE FRECKLES SCATTERED ALL OVER YOUR SOFT SKIN: THEY SHINE WITH THE PROVOCATION OF DISTANCE."
THEN HE WENT TO SLEEP.
IN THE MORNING, HE SAW SHE HAD MESSAGED HIM.
"YOU STILL AWAKE?" SHE HAD WRITTEN.
HE SMILED, AND RESPONDED: "I FELL ASLEEP! DID YOU NEED SOMETHING?"
"I WANTED TO TALK TO YOU SINCE YOU CLAIM TO NEVER SLEEP!" SHE ANSWERED."
"SLEEP IS A WASTE OF TIME. BUT SOMETIMES I FALL ASLEEP UNINTENTIONALLY!

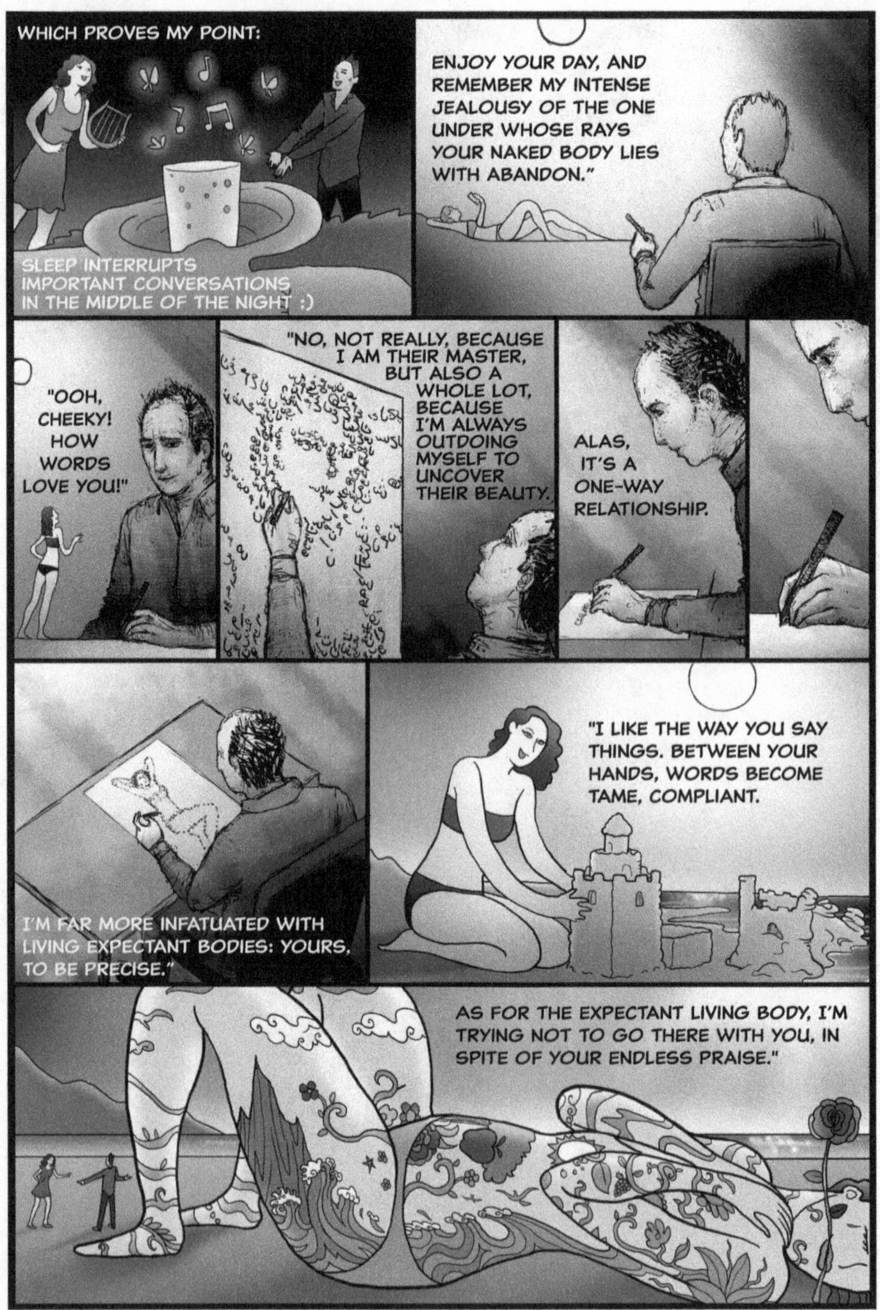
WHICH PROVES MY POINT:
SLEEP INTERRUPTS IMPORTANT CONVERSATIONS IN THE MIDDLE OF THE NIGHT :)
ENJOY YOUR DAY, AND REMEMBER MY INTENSE JEALOUSY OF THE ONE UNDER WHOSE RAYS YOUR NAKED BODY LIES WITH ABANDON."
"OOH, CHEEKY! HOW WORDS LOVE YOU!"
"NO, NOT REALLY, BECAUSE I AM THEIR MASTER, BUT ALSO A WHOLE LOT, BECAUSE I'M ALWAYS OUTDOING MYSELF TO UNCOVER THEIR BEAUTY.
ALAS, IT'S A ONE-WAY RELATIONSHIP.
I'M FAR MORE INFATUATED WITH LIVING EXPECTANT BODIES: YOURS, TO BE PRECISE."
"I LIKE THE WAY YOU SAY THINGS. BETWEEN YOUR HANDS, WORDS BECOME TAME, COMPLIANT.
AS FOR THE EXPECTANT LIVING BODY, I'M TRYING NOT TO GO THERE WITH YOU, IN SPITE OF YOUR ENDLESS PRAISE."

"IN THAT CASE, YOU WILL MISS THE FANTASTIC FEELING OF TWO CONSUMMATELY BEAUTIFUL ENTITIES COLLIDING.
"YOU WILL BE THE KILLJOY THAT EXTINGUISHES THE RESULTANT SPARKS. THAT'S A HEAVY RESPONSIBILITY!"
"I KNOW! BUT I'M JUST FOLLOWING YOUR INSTRUCTIONS."
I HAD TOLD HER RIGHT FROM THE GET-GO THAT I WAS A COMPLICATED GUY, THAT IT WOULD BE HARD TO HAVE A "NORMAL" RELATIONSHIP WITH ME. IF YOU'RE NOT THE SORT OF PERSON THAT LIKES TO PLAY WITH FIRE, LIKE A MOTH, THEN GET AWAY FROM MY ARDOR, I SAID.
HONESTLY, I TELL THEM ALL THE SAME THING, AND RIGHT FROM THE VERY BEGINNING, SO AS TO PRECLUDE THE POSSIBILITY OF THEIR FEELING DISAPPOINTED OR DECEIVED.

"I AM WHO I AM AND YOU ARE WHO YOU ARE: IF WE CANNOT BE FREE TOGETHER AND FREE OF EACH OTHER, THERE'S NO NEED TO GO ANY FURTHER.
ALL I WANT IS TO EXERCISE MY FREEDOM, AS I SEE IT, TO THE UTMOST EXTENT. INCLUDING MY FREEDOM FROM YOU. AND THE CONVERSE AS WELL: I DON'T WANT TO WEIGH YOU DOWN OR INCUR SOME KIND...
...OF OBLIGATION ON YOUR PART, NOR DO I WANT TO BE AN APPARATUS OF SURVEILLANCE."
MANY PRACTICE LOVE AS A POSSESSIVE AND OBSESSIVE UNDERTAKING—IT'S A BOND, A FORM OF OBLIGATION. WHEN "CROWNING" THEIR LOVE WITH MARRIAGE, LOVERS SAY, "LET US TIE THE KNOT."
THE KNOT A CROWN! FOR ME, LOVE IS THE EXACT OPPOSITE: IT IS TOTAL FREEDOM. I SAY, LET US UNTIE THE KNOT, LET US UNTIE ALL KNOTS. THE PERSON WHO LOVES ME IS THE ONE WHO URGES ME TO LIBERATION, WHO PROPELS ME TO FREEDOM.
THERE I GO TALKING TOO MUCH AGAIN. I'LL JUST SEND HER A ONE-LINER.
SMS CHAT SESSION 2
"I SURRENDER THEN :-)"
"WHAT? YOU DON'T WANT TO CONVINCE ME OF THE BEAUTY OF COLLIDING BODIES?! ;)"

"CONVINCE YOU? THE COLLISION I'M TALKING ABOUT IS THE ENCOUNTER OF FREE BODIES, BODIES THAT MOVE OF THEIR OWN VOLITION,
MEANING THAT YOU TOO HAVE TO EXPRESS YOUR DESIRE FOR ME. I'M NOT GOING TO KISS YOUR ASS—DESIRABLE AS IT MAY BE!"
"I DON'T EXPECT THINGS AROUND ME TO HAPPEN JUST LIKE THAT, I MAKE THEM HAPPEN. SO, IF COLLISION THERE IS TO BE, I'M NOT GOING TO BE ADVERTISING IT!"
"I'M HERE, ON THE TUMULTUOUS PATH LEADING TO COLLISION, WAITING."
TWO DAYS WENT BY, THEN TWO WEEKS. AND THEN TWO WHOLE MONTHS. NOTHING. THE TUMULTUOUS PATH TO COLLISION REMAINED UNTRODDEN.
HIS WORDS, HIS ARDOR, HIS ACERBIC WIT, AND HIS NO-HOLDS-BARRED TAKE ON LIFE MAKE ME MELT INSIDE. HE IS COMPLETELY UNVARNISHED, TELLING IT LIKE IT IS, WITHOUT ANY SUGARCOATING. LIKE AN X-RAY THAT PENETRATES EVERY LAYER AND SEES RIGHT THROUGH EACH AND EVERY ONE; HE CALLS A SPADE A SPADE.
"THE TRUTH IS NOT TO BE KNOWN ONLY BUT TO BE TOLD," HE LIKES TO SAY, QUOTING SHEBLI SHMAYYEL.

HE READS WHAT I WRITE CLOSELY, AND HE FILLS THE PAGES WITH ARROWS AND COMMENTS. HE'S ALWAYS LOOKING OUT FOR A UNIVERSITY SCHOLARSHIP I COULD APPLY FOR. "HERE'S ONE TO ITALY," HE EMAILS ME. IT LOOKS LIKE IT'S RIGHT UP YOUR ALLEY. CLICK ON THE LINK BELOW! ENJOY!" HE GIFTS ME POETRY AND MUSIC,
AND HOLDS ME TENDERLY. WHAT CAN I SAY?
BUT THIS OPAQUE BARRIER REMAINS, A CONSTANT QUESTION I COME UP AGAINST WHENEVER I TRY TO GET UNDER HIS SKIN.
THE QUESTION OF THE FUTURE, YOU KNOW, OF SETTLING DOWN. I KNOW THE WORD IS FULL OF TRADITIONALIST OVERTONES,
BUT IT FEELS REAL AND CLOSE TO THE BONE.
HE'D TELL ME THAT SETTLING DOWN WAS A FEATURE THAT DEVELOPED FROM A LONG FEMALE HISTORY OF NATURAL SELECTION. AFTER A GLASS OF HIS FAVORITE RED WINE,
WHEN HE'S A LITTLE MELLOW, HE CHUCKLES: "IT'S NOT BAD ENOUGH THAT GOD IS PATRIARCHAL,
EVEN MOTHER NATURE EXHIBITS MASCULINIST TENDENCIES!"
WHEN I ASK HIM WHAT HE MEANS, HIS FACE LIGHTS UP: "HUMAN SOCIETIES KNOW THAT ENDOGAMY—MARRIAGE WITHIN A GROUP—LEADS TO GENETIC MUTATIONS AND CRETINISM
ERROR
EXOGAMY IS CLEARLY SUPERIOR AS IT BASICALLY DIVERSIFIES THE GENE POOL, AND HUMANKIND HAS KNOWN THAT SIMPLE FACT SINCE THE DAWN OF TIME.

MEN INCLINED TO DIVERSIFYING THE GENE POOL HAD LIVES THAT WERE FULL OF CHILDREN—WHICH IS HOW THE DIVERSIFIERS SURVIVED AND THEIR FAITHLESS WAYS WON—
WHILE FAITHFUL MEN WHO EMBRACED MONOGAMY BECAME EXTINCT!
FOR WOMEN, THE REVERSE WAS TRUE: THOSE THAT TENDED TOWARDS STABILITY AND ROOTEDNESS WERE BETTER ABLE TO CARE FOR THEIR CHILDREN, WHO THEN SURVIVED IN GREATER NUMBERS. THAT IS HOW THE SETTLED OR STABLE ONES SURVIVED, ALONG WITH THEIR LOYAL WAYS AND CIRCUMSCRIBED SEXUAL CHOICES
—AND THOSE THAT HOPPED HEEDLESSLY FROM ONE GUY TO ANOTHER BECAME EXTINCT!
THAT, MY DEAR, IS THE EVIDENCE THAT NATURE CONSPIRES WITH MEN FOR THEIR ENJOYMENT ... AND THAT IT IS NATURE—
AND NOT CAPITALISM—WHICH CAME UP WITH THE FIRST DIVISION OF LABOR!" HE SAYS.
"I'M JUST TELLING IT LIKE IT IS!" HE ADDS, LAUGHING SO HARD THAT TEARS STREAM DOWN HIS CHEEKS.
BULLSHIT. I WASN'T CONVINCED BY ALL THAT PONTIFICATION. DAMNED MEN, CALLING THE SHOTS IN PHILOSOPHY, SCIENCE, AND RELIGION SINCE THE DAWN OF WRITTEN HISTORY.
AND I DON'T CARE THAT HE MOCKED ME IN AN UNDERHANDED WAY.
I REALLY DON'T THINK THAT WANTING TO SETTLE DOWN, EVEN IN THE TRADITIONAL SENSE OF THE
WORD, IS SOME KIND OF DEFICIENCY.

I OFTEN FEEL SOMETHING STIRRING IN MY GUT, AS IF MY WOMB WERE ITCHING FROM THE INSIDE SAYING,
I WANT A CHILD, A CHILD THAT COMES OUT OF ME. I WANT TO GIVE LIFE, TO CREATE. BUT HE DOESN'T UNDERSTAND ANY OF THAT.
HOW CAN SOMEONE WHO EJACULATES HUNDREDS OF MILLIONS OF SPERM THAT COMPETE WITH ONE ANOTHER OVER ONE OVUM,
WITH ONLY ONE OF THEM MAKING IT WHILE ALL THE REST DIE, UNDERSTAND? HUNDREDS OF MILLIONS AGAINST ONE. MILLIONS OF DEATHS FOR ONE LIFE. MALE AND FEMALE PITTED AGAINST EACH OTHER.
AND THIS LIFE, THIS SINGLE EGG, NEEDS NURTURE AND CARE ...AND STABILITY.
HOW CAN HE UNDERSTAND THAT?
THE WOMB, THAT INNER COCOON,
IS LIKE A TENDER EMBRACE.
BUT THE PENIS, ON THE OUTSIDE, IS MORE AKIN TO A ROCKET THAT SHOOTS UP INTO THE AIR AND CLEAVES AWAY FROM
THE SOIL OF THE BODY.
THE OVUM IS A PEARL IN AN OYSTER SHELL,
AND SEMEN A SPRAY OF WATER FROM A GARDENING HOSE.

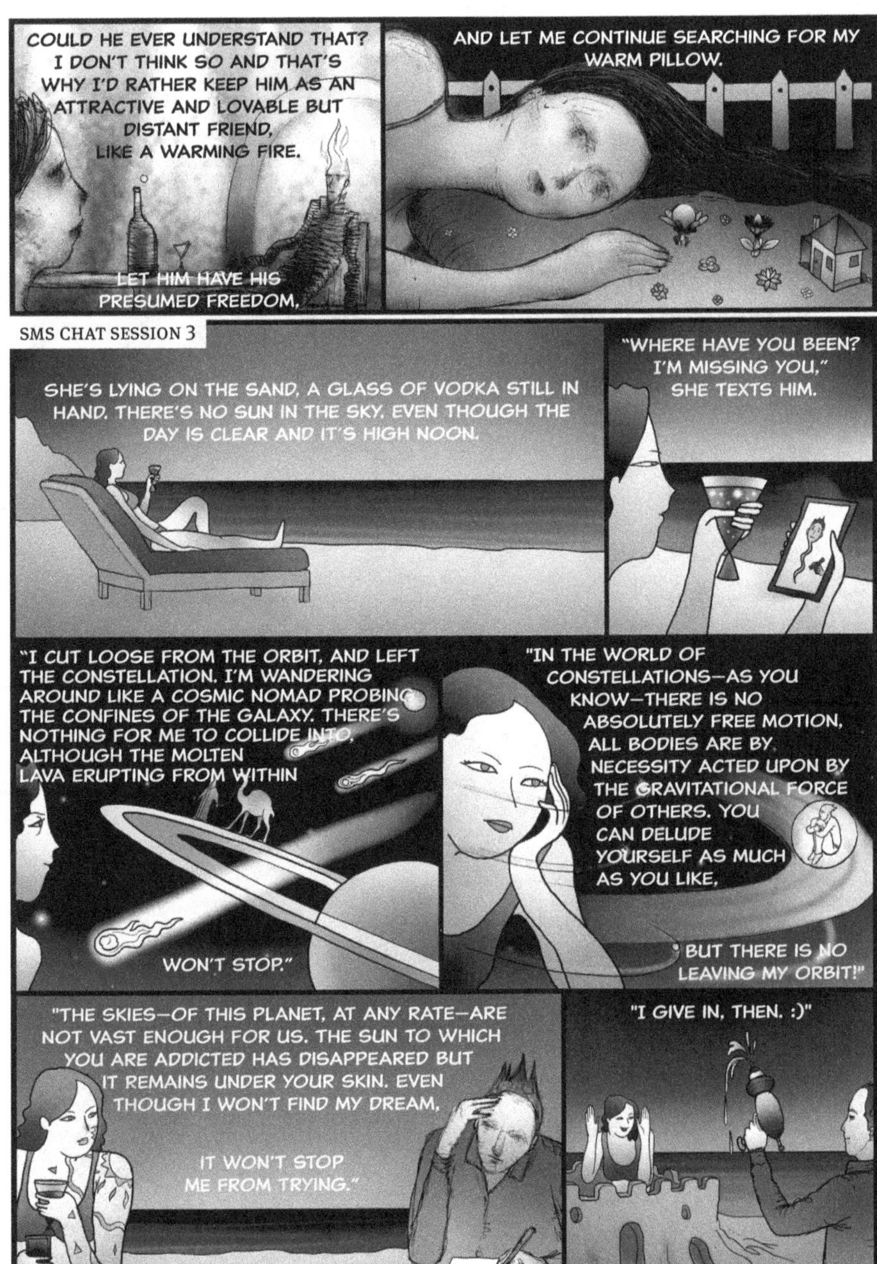
COULD HE EVER UNDERSTAND THAT? I DON'T THINK SO AND THAT'S WHY I'D RATHER KEEP HIM AS AN ATTRACTIVE AND LOVABLE BUT DISTANT FRIEND, LIKE A WARMING FIRE.
LET HIM HAVE HIS PRESUMED FREEDOM,
AND LET ME CONTINUE SEARCHING FOR MY WARM PILLOW.
SMS CHAT SESSION 3
SHE'S LYING ON THE SAND, A GLASS OF VODKA STILL IN HAND. THERE'S NO SUN IN THE SKY, EVEN THOUGH THE DAY IS CLEAR AND IT'S HIGH NOON.
"WHERE HAVE YOU BEEN? I'M MISSING YOU," SHE TEXTS HIM.
"I CUT LOOSE FROM THE ORBIT, AND LEFT THE CONSTELLATION. I'M WANDERING AROUND LIKE A COSMIC NOMAD PROBING THE CONFINES OF THE GALAXY. THERE'S NOTHING FOR ME TO COLLIDE INTO, ALTHOUGH THE MOLTEN LAVA ERUPTING FROM WITHIN
WON'T STOP."
"IN THE WORLD OF CONSTELLATIONS—AS YOU KNOW—THERE IS NO ABSOLUTELY FREE MOTION, ALL BODIES ARE BY NECESSITY ACTED UPON BY THE GRAVITATIONAL FORCE OF OTHERS. YOU CAN DELUDE YOURSELF AS MUCH AS YOU LIKE,
BUT THERE IS NO LEAVING MY ORBIT!"
"THE SKIES—OF THIS PLANET, AT ANY RATE—ARE NOT VAST ENOUGH FOR US. THE SUN TO WHICH YOU ARE ADDICTED HAS DISAPPEARED BUT IT REMAINS UNDER YOUR SKIN. EVEN THOUGH I WON'T FIND MY DREAM,
IT WON'T STOP ME FROM TRYING."
"I GIVE IN, THEN. :)"

THE WOMB OF THE UNIVERSE. THE ONE AND ONLY STABLE, COMPRESSED MASS. WITH NO VOLUME, ETERNALLY DENSE, OUTSIDE TIME OR SPACE.

SOMETHING HAPPENS. NO ONE KNOWS WHAT IT IS PRECISELY. SOME KIND OF FERTILIZATION OCCURS,

MATTER ERUPTS AND SCATTERS, TIME STARTS,

AND AS THE PARTS SEPARATE,

SPACE GROWS.

IN THE BEGINNING, DISORDER
EMERGED FROM STASIS.
AND NOW, AFTER BILLIONS OF YEARS,
ON A TINY LITTLE PLANET ORBITING A STAR ON THE ARM OF A GALAXY...
...WITH THOUSANDS OF STARS IN A UNIVERSE
THAT HAS BILLIONS
OF GALAXIES,
WE WATCH HER WALKING
SLOWLY ON THE SAND,
HER LIGHT-SKINNED BODY
COVERED BY NOTHING
MORE THAN MINISCULE
PIECES OF CLOTH THAT
CONSUME THE ONE
OBSERVING HER.
SOMETHING IS
STIRRING IN HER
GUT, IS IT THE
VODKA?
PROBABLY NOT.

FROM HER PURSE, SHE TAKES OUT THE STRIP OF CONTRACEPTIVE PILLS SHE BOUGHT A WEEK BEFORE THE DAY THE BED BROKE UNDER THEM...
...ALL OF THE COLORED PILLS SMILING IN THEIR LITTLE BUBBLES, NOT A SINGLE ONE IS MISSING.
SHE SMILES BACK AT THEM,
BIDDING THEM *GOODBYE* AS SHE TOSSES THE STRIP INTO A TRASHCAN ALONG THE WALKWAY,
AND PROCEEDS TO HER ROOM,
STEPPING LIGHTLY AS THE PURPLE SUN SETS INTO A CRIMSON RED SEA.

ACKNOWLEDGEMENTS

Stories from this book have appeared in different formats in the following literary reviews and anthologies: *The Los Angeles Review of Books Quarterly*, *Dust*, *3:AM*, *The Punch*, *Newfound*, *The Best Asian Short Stories*, *TSS Publishing*, *Rusted Radishes*, *Moon City Review*, *Hotel*, *Barricade*, *ArabLit Quarterly*, *The Radiance of the Short Story: Fiction from Around the Globe*, *Ponder Review*, *Prototype 2* and *Hawai'i Review*.

The author wishes to thank the editors of all those literary publications and anthologies for their editorial comments and contributions.

The author wishes to thank his translator maia tabet for her exceptional work and patience with lengthy and detailed discussions over several drafts of each story.

ABOUT THE AUTHOR

Hisham Bustani is an award-winning Jordanian author of five collections of short fiction and poetry. He is acclaimed for his bold style and unique narrative voice, and often experiments with the boundaries of short fiction and prose poetry. Much of his work revolves around issues related to social and political change, particularly the dystopian experience of post-colonial modernity in the Arab world. His work has been described as "bringing a new wave of surrealism to [Arabic] literary culture, which missed the surrealist revolution of the last century," and it has been said that he "belongs to an angry new Arab generation. Indeed, he is at the forefront of this generation—combining an unbounded modernist literary sensibility with a vision for total change.... His anger extends to encompass everything, including literary conventions." Hisham's fiction and poetry have been translated into many languages, with English-language translations appearing in prestigious journals across the United States, United Kingdom, and Canada, including *The Kenyon Review*, *Black Warrior Review*, *The Georgia Review*, *The Poetry Review*, *Modern Poetry in Translation*, *World Literature Today*, and *The Los Angeles Review of Books Quarterly*. His fiction has been featured in *The*

Best Asian Short Stories, *The Ordinary Chaos of Being Human: Tales from Many Muslim Worlds*, *The Radiance of the Short Story: Fiction from Around the Globe*, *Influence and Confluence—East and West: A Global Anthology on the Short Story* among other anthologies. In 2009, he was selected by the German review *Inamo* as one of the Arab world's emerging and influential new writers. In 2013, the U.K.-based webzine *The Culture Trip* listed him as one of Jordan's top six contemporary writers. Hisham's *The Perception of Meaning* (Syracuse University Press, 2015) won the University of Arkansas Arabic Translation Award. Hisham is the Arabic fiction editor of the Amherst College-based literary review *The Common*, and was the 2017 recipient of the Rockefeller Foundation's Bellagio Fellowship for Artists and Writers.

ABOUT THE TRANSLATOR

maia tabet is an Arabic-English literary translator based in Washington DC, where she is the associate editor of the *Journal of Palestine Studies*. She is the translator of *Little Mountain* and *White Masks* by Elias Khoury, and of the 2010 International Prize for Arabic Fiction (IPAF), *Throwing Sparks*, by Abdo Khal. Her translation of Sinan Antoon's *The Baghdad Eucharist* (*Ya Mariam*, in Arabic) appeared in Spring 2017. Her translations of both fiction and non-fiction have been widely published in journals, literary reviews, and other media, including *Barricade*, *The Common*, *Words Without Borders*, *Portal 9*, *Fikrun wa Fann*, and the *Journal of Palestine Studies*. She is currently at work on her fifth novel-length translation.

OTHER TITLES FROM MASON JAR PRESS

Peculiar Heritage
poetry DeMisty D. Bellinger

Call a Body Home
short stories chapbook by Michael Alessi

The Horror is Us
an anthology of horror fiction edited by Justin Sanders

Suppose Muscle Suppose Night Suppose This in August
memoir by Danielle Zaccagnino

Ashley Sugarnotch & the Wolf
poetry by Elizabeth Deanna Morris Lakes

...and Other Disasters
short stories by Malka Older

All Friends Are Necessary
a novella by Tomas Moniz

Continental Breakfast
poetry by Danny Caine

How to Sit
memoir by Tyrese Coleman

Learn more at masonjarpress.com

CPSIA information can be obtained
at www.ICGtesting.com
Printed in the USA
BVHW081411120122
625992BV00009B/297